The world is in peril.

An ancient evil is rising from beneath Erdas, and we need YOU to help stop it.

Claim your spirit animal and join the adventure now:

1. Go to scholastic.com/spiritanimals.

2. Log in to create your character and choose your own spirit animal.

3. Have your book ready and enter the code below to unlock the adventure.

Your code: NXH9NPFNXG

By the Four Fallen,
The Greencloaks

scholastic.com/spiritanimals

Treat these strangers
with caution.

We don't know if they
are friends or foes.

BROKEN
GROUND

Victoria Schwab

SCHOLASTIC INC.

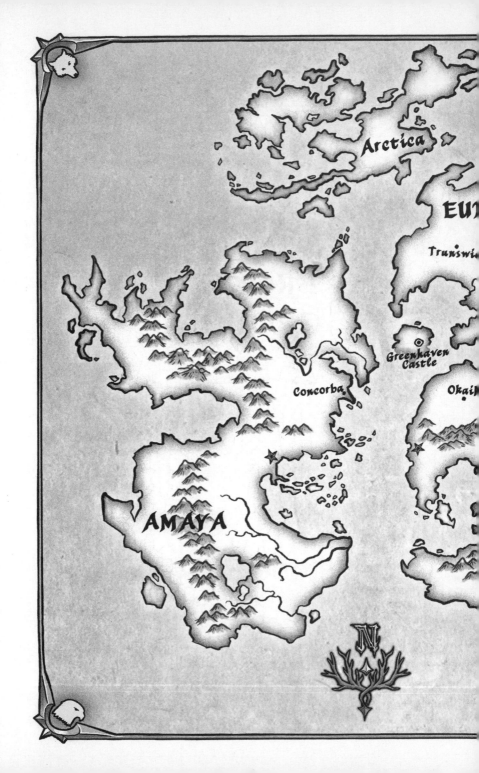

Library of Congress Control Number: 2015950270
ISBN 978-0-545-85442-9

10 9 8 7 6 5 4 3 2 1   16 17 18 19 20

Book design by Charice Silverman
First edition, January 2016

Printed in the U.S.A. 23

Scholastic US: 557 Broadway • New York, NY 10012
Scholastic Canada: 604 King Street West • Toronto, ON M5V 1E1
Scholastic New Zealand Limited: Private Bag 94407 • Greenmount, Manukau 2141
Scholastic UK Ltd.: Euston House • 24 Eversholt Street • London NW1 1DB

SHADOWS IN STETRIOL

CLOUDS RAKED ACROSS THE SKY, BLOTTING OUT THE MOON and stars.

It was not a night for looking up.

If it had been, someone in Stetriol might have seen the shadows slipping over the rooftops, the shapes perched like gargoyles atop the walls. Someone might have seen the young man standing at the peak of a roof like a weathervane, his face hidden behind a pale, horned mask, his dark cloak snapping in the breeze. But all eyes were down, focused on books and hearths, meals and fires and drinks, and no one noticed.

The figure straightened and began to walk lithely along the spines of the shingled roofs, the cloak billowing behind him. In the color-stripped night, the cloak looked black, but when he paused and the lamplight flickered up from the roads and courtyards below and caught the fabric, it shone *red*.

All around him, Stetriol was alive in a way it hadn't been in ages. The city had a pulse again, and it was beating, beating, beating in time with his heart, his steps.

The streets fell away below him as he moved with animal grace over the tops of shops and houses until he found the one he was looking for. He paused against a chimney, then sank into a crouch, the horns of his mask catching the light before vanishing with the rest of him into shadow.

In a courtyard below, a girl sat on the rim of a fountain, her long white-blond hair twisted up around her head like a crown. Her legs swished absently in the shallow pool, where a large swan drifted, its feathers as white as sunlight on snow. Behind the horned mask, the young man's eyes—not human eyes, but slit sideways, like a ram's—widened at the sight of the animal, and he leaned forward at an almost impossible angle, entranced as the swan slid gracefully over the water's surface.

So the rumors were true.

Ninani had come to Stetriol.

The girl's hair and the swan's feathers made twin pools of pale white light against the muted greens and blues and shadow grays of the courtyard. The girl had a book open and was reading aloud to the swan, her voice soft and sweet, the words lost beneath the gentle swish of the water around her legs.

Back on the rooftop, a flash of movement caught the man's eyes; another cloaked figure appeared on the opposite wall of the courtyard, only the snout of a coyote mask visible against the slated roof. Howl. The canine figure shifted his weight; on the ground, he was unstoppable, but he'd never been comfortable with heights.

Howl, the first signed in greeting.

Stead, the second signed back.

A third cloaked shadow sprang out of the darkness to Howl's right, a feline smile carved into the mask that hid her face, her movements so smooth he hadn't even noticed her approach.

Shadow.

The girl signed a dismissive hello, then sank into a crouch and steadied herself on the roof, her nails glinting, curved and sharp as a cat's.

The three perched like stone statues above the court-yard, surrounding the girl and her spirit animal as she read on, unaware of their presence. Howl shifted his footing a second time.

What now? signed Shadow, her fingers dancing lazily through the air.

The young man in the horned mask—*Stead*, they called him—squinted, and then signed his command. *Send word to King.*

Shadow drew a finger around her head in answer. The sign for horns was the same as the one for crown. They had wanted to call him that. *Crown.* He was, after all, King's second-in-command. But the gesture made Stead uncomfortable—his loyalty to their leader was absolute, unflinching—so he'd opted for Stead. As in *steadfast* or *steady-on-your-feet*.

He waved Shadow's tease away.

Below, the girl trailed off and went to turn the page when the book slipped from her hands. She fumbled with it, but it fell, bounced off her knee, and landed with a splash in the fountain.

The swan bristled, fluttering her wings.

"Oops," whispered the girl, dragging the sodden book out of the water. She held it up by one corner, and sighed as water dripped from the pages. "Don't tell Father."

She set the book aside; it landed with a soft wet smack on the fountain's edge.

Just then, Howl shifted his footing a third time, and slipped.

A loose tile beneath his boot came free and went skittering down the peak of the roof. Howl managed to catch himself against the nearest chimney, but he was too late to save the tile. It rocketed forward toward the edge of the roof and the courtyard below. Stead recoiled, back pressed against the chimney, already braced for the crash, but Shadow lunged, body arcing gracefully, and caught the slate with a claw-like nail before it could plummet down to the courtyard floor.

Mortar pebbles skittered down the roof and over the edge, as soft as rain.

The cloaked figures held their breath.

Below, the swan stilled in her pool.

The girl looked up, but it was dark above the lanterns. "What was that?" she asked softly. She and the swan both craned their necks. The girl squinted, as if she could *almost* see the outline of a figure, the edge of a mask.

"Tasha!" called a voice from within the house. The girl's attention wavered, drifted back down to the fountain and the house behind her.

"Must have been a bird," said the girl. "Or a mouse. Or the wind." She swung her legs out of the water, and then trailed her fingers through its glassy surface.

"Come on, Ninani," she said pleasantly.

The swan fluttered for a moment, lifting her wings as if about to take flight, before disappearing in a flash of light. As she vanished, a mark appeared, black as ink against the girl's fair skin, a swan wrapping from wrist to elbow. With that the girl padded inside, leaving a trail of damp footprints in her wake.

Tasha. So that was her name.

The moment she was gone, the feline Shadow uncoiled and hauled herself upright on the roof. Her usually green eyes were black, the pupils blown out in the low light, and they glared daggers at Howl. She looked as if she planned to chuck the discarded tile at his head.

"Idiot," she hissed aloud.

"We weren't all meant for scaling buildings," he growled in return.

"Enough," ordered Stead, his voice low and even. Howl and Shadow both drew breath, as if about to go on, when Stead's hand shot up in warning.

A sound, like the shuffle of bare feet on stone.

An instant later Tasha hurried back out into the courtyard to retrieve the book she'd left on the fountain's edge. Halfway there, she caught her foot on a mat, and nearly stumbled before righting herself and taking up the sodden book. She pressed the covers together to squeeze out the last of the water and turned back toward the house.

And stopped.

She hesitated, cast a last look at the rooftops and the night sky above.

"Tasha!" called the voice again.

And then the girl was gone, retreating back inside.

When the courtyard had been still for several moments, Stead made a signal with one hand, a silent command to retreat. Shadow set the roof tile against the nearest chimney, and she and Howl peeled away, vanishing into the dark. He watched them go with his sharp, slit gold eyes, and then looked back at the courtyard, the damp footprints already beginning to disappear.

Tasha.

They knew where she was now.

Where *Ninani* was.

And they would be back.

With that, Stead slipped away and followed the others into shadow and night.

EYES IN THE DARK

THE TORCHLIGHT MADE THEIR SHADOWS DANCE.

They walked through the tunnels below the world, casting a train of eerie silhouettes, all stretched out and flickering against the cave walls. Conor tried to focus on the people instead of their monstrous shadows, but he couldn't stop his eyes from wandering to the rock walls, where their distorted versions twisted and hovered. Meilin, Takoda, and Xanthe were nothing but spindly forms. Briggan's shadow was low, all ears and tail.

But it was Kovo's that disturbed him most.

The ape's shadow stretched and loomed, towering over the others with its teeth bared. In the haunting, unsteady light, Conor thought he could even see the beast's red eyes glowing impossibly in the shadow's warping face.

Conor swallowed and squeezed his eyes shut, trying to separate what was real from what was fever and fatigue. More and more, the two blurred together in his sight. The edges weren't sharp, and if he didn't focus, the nightmares could slip so easily out of his dreams and into the darkened tunnels around them.

"Are you sure you know where you're going?" asked Meilin—the *real* Meilin, not shadow but flesh and blood and stern resolve—from the path ahead. She was gripping the torchlight, angling its beam from the pale pink eyes of the other girl, the one who was leading the group through the underground maze.

"I'm sure," said Xanthe.

"How can you be sure?" muttered Meilin. "Everything looks the same . . ."

"Maybe to you," said Xanthe simply, running a delicate hand along the wall.

But it looked the same to Conor, too. Now and then he could feel the ground beneath them slope slightly downward, could feel the air get a fraction warmer or colder, a strange current like the breath of a sleeping beast. But otherwise, the tangled tunnels of Sadre did all look the same. An endless repetition of caves and caverns and tunnels. He felt like they were going in circles. *Spirals.*

How could Xanthe possibly know where they were going? And yet, she seemed to.

They came to a kind of crossroads in the tunnel. The three paths, one ahead and one to either side, looked identical. Xanthe held up a hand for them to stop, while she alone continued forward to the very center of the intersection. She readjusted the pack on her shoulder and knelt, laying her hands flat against the stone, and closing her eyes. Conor didn't know if she was listening or feeling or smelling or using some other sense he didn't have. All he knew was that, when she opened her eyes a few seconds later and straightened, she gestured to the tunnel on the left.

"This way," she said, continuing on without even looking back.

Kovo and Meilin each let out a skeptical sound, something between a sigh and a grunt, then shot dark looks at each other. Takoda chuckled, and even Conor managed a smile. It wasn't the first time the two had behaved alike. Meilin might have summoned Jhi the Panda, the picture of serenity, but she was as stubborn as the ape when she wanted to be.

Meilin strode after Xanthe, and Takoda and Kovo fell in step behind.

Now that he'd stopped, Conor's body felt sluggish, detached, and he struggled to make it move again. When the others had entered the tunnel and he had not, Briggan's muzzle found his thigh, nudging him forward. The gesture was small, but enough to coax his legs into motion.

"Thanks," he whispered tiredly, running a hand along the wolf's scruff. Briggan leaned against his leg, not hard enough to set him off balance. Just enough to show Conor that he could lean on him, too.

"It's not magic," Xanthe was saying when Conor caught up.

"Then how do you do it?" asked Meilin. "How do you know which way to go?"

"I listen to the caves," answered Xanthe, as if this explained it.

"Will you teach me?" pressed Meilin, and Conor wondered if her insistence was because she didn't think Xanthe really knew where they were going, or if Meilin simply didn't like relying on anyone else for help. Probably both.

Xanthe chewed her lip. "I don't think I can teach you," she said. "I know because I have always known. And I have always known because I *need* to know."

Meilin frowned. "Well, that is both mysterious and entirely unhelpful."

"Sorry."

Takoda, who'd been busy trying to teach Kovo how to sign a *question* instead of a *statement*—and having no success—looked up. "So everyone down here knows how to find their way?"

"Not everyone," said Xanthe, stepping up and over a low rock, and holding a few tendrils of mossy rope out of the way so they could pass. "When the children in Sadre are—were—old enough to walk, our mothers and fathers would take us to a place in the caves, somewhere close to our homes, and leave us."

Meilin let out a short gasp. "That's awful."

Xanthe shrugged. "It wasn't far, and almost all the children could find their way back."

Almost all, thought Conor grimly. And what of those who couldn't? He'd seen animals in the wild abandon their young, focus their time and energy on those strong enough to survive.

"The next year," continued Xanthe, skirting a crumbled section of wall, "the parents would take the children farther, somewhere with a few twists or turns, but still not *too* many dangers, and they would return home to wait. Every year, the children were taken somewhere and left to find their way, and every year, the path got harder, the pitfalls more precarious. Parents would spend all year teaching their children about the caves—how to make light, how to find food, which water was safe to drink, which mushrooms were edible and which were toxic, how to tell where you were from the direction of the markings left by water in the rocks—to help them survive that one day. Every year . . ." Xanthe trailed off, lost in her own thoughts. Perhaps in memories of Phos Astos and the family she'd lost.

When Xanthe spoke again, she was smiling, but her voice was laced with sadness. "So no," she said apologetically. "I don't think I can teach you."

Meilin stared at the girl with a look Conor had rarely seen before on the warrior from Zhong. He thought it might be respect. Or awe. Takoda's mouth was open. Even Kovo's face was steady with appraisal.

The tunnels around them were changing again, oscillating. Their ceilings and sides rose and fell in a way that made Conor's head swim. He felt himself stumble once, then again, over loose rocks. The second time, he stuck out his hand and caught himself against an outcrop, the wall's texture strange and chalky against his hand.

The stone was darker here, flaking like charred coal under his touch and smudging on his skin. A drop of sweat ran down his cheek and landed on his palm, turning the black ash into ink. He shuddered, feeling unwell, but straightened and forced himself to follow.

"Watch your step," called Xanthe, treading gingerly around a hole in the center of the floor.

Conor wouldn't have noticed it. Even knowing it was there, he nearly fell, and then he realized, too late, that it wasn't clumsiness or fatigue slowing him down, weakening his limbs and robbing him of balance.

It was the parasite working its way through his body.

Panic rippled through him. He'd wanted to forget so badly that he almost had. Now the remembering hit him like a blow. His skin was burning, but his blood felt icy in his veins. The shiver, once an occasional thing, was now constant, a tremor that followed him through the days—if they could be called days in a place without sun—and into fevered sleep.

Briggan padded along beside him, his body a simple reassuring presence in the dark. Conor curled his fingers in the wolf's fur, then recoiled as he felt the parasite shift beneath his skin.

A voice—like water over rocks—whispered through his head.

Xanthe glanced over her shoulder at Conor, and he fought back a shudder. Her pale skin, white hair, pink eyes, suddenly reminded him of the Many, those horrible creatures that had somehow once been human, and were now only *things*. And soon, too soon, Conor would be one, too.

Was there anything left of the Many but teeth and nails and horror?

What would be left of *him*?

The only physical difference between him and them was the dark spiral that marked their foreheads, and once the parasite finished its slow trek through his body, it would leave that mark on him, too.

How far had it spread?

He didn't want to see.

Didn't want to know.

But he had to.

Conor bit his cheek and slid the fabric of his sleeve up to his elbow. The last time he'd checked, days before, the spiraled tip of the mark stopped there, in the crook of his arm. He'd marked it with his nail, scratching a thin red line to note the parasite's progress. The line was still there, but the streak of black had vanished beneath his shirt-sleeve. It was still moving, and Conor could only imagine the path it would take up toward his shoulder, his throat, his cheek, his forehead. He gripped his forearm until it ached, until his fingers left bruises on the skin. But it did nothing to stop the thing moving through him, just as it couldn't stop the whispers starting in his head, as soft and steady as a distant stream. Words muffled like voices beyond a door. Words he couldn't understand, and didn't want to.

Conor shook his head, trying to push away the voices, the image of the Many, the fear, and to remind himself that he still had a chance, still had time. If they could get to the Wyrm before the Evertree died, if they could defeat the age-old creature, if winning could save the infected, if, if, if . . .

Briggan looked up at him, his blue canine eyes wise and worried.

"It's okay," said Conor, trying to still the tremor in his voice, to sound calm and soothing, the way he did when he spoke to his sheep so long ago, when he was just a shepherd. Not a boy famous for summoning one of the Great Beasts. "We'll be okay."

Conor had always tried to tell the truth. He knew this was a lie, but he so badly wanted it to be true.

"What's it like?" asked Takoda ahead, navigating the uneven ground with lithe steps that reminded Conor of Abeke's grace. "Living in the dark?"

Xanthe shot him a smile. "I don't know," she answered. "What's it like, living in the light?"

Takoda laughed softly. His blue monastery robes billowed behind him, now dingy from their trek through Sadre. "Fair enough. But how do things grow? Do you know what birdsong sounds like? What is—"

Xanthe laughed and held up her hands. "Slow down there. First of all, light isn't the only source of nourishment. We have vegetables—carrots, potatoes, yucca—that thrive in the dark, and herbs that feed on the minerals in the rocks, and fungi that make their own light, and rocks that can spark fires. And your birds make song? Ours make sounds, but I wouldn't call it music. More of a squeak. What do birds sound like above?"

Takoda brought his hands together and whistled into them, making a kind of melodic trill that echoed through the caves around them. Xanthe broke into a smile. Kovo scowled. The ape had been signing something at Takoda for several long seconds, but the boy's back was turned, his attention on Xanthe. Finally, the Great Beast reached out and knocked him in the shoulder. Takoda would have tripped, had the ape's fist not been tangled in the boy's robes. Satisfied that he had the boy's attention, Kovo signed again, slowly, deliberately, adding a snort of displeasure to the end like a punctuation mark.

Conor didn't know what the ape was saying, but Takoda frowned a little, then wrested himself free. "I don't know," he said. "Maybe if you phrased it as a question or—"

But that obviously *wasn't* the answer the ape wanted, because his lips curled back, teeth bared. Takoda rolled his eyes and turned toward Xanthe. "Kovo wants to know how much farther we have to go. He doesn't like it down here."

"That makes two of us," said Meilin.

Conor was about to say *three* when his foot landed on something slick and he started to fall, not down but *through*. A thin layer of chalky ground gave way beneath his shoe. And then, abruptly, he stopped falling. Not because the hole was shallow—no, it plummeted down and away into nothing but blackness—but because something had caught his elbow. A massive hand encircled his arm, and he looked up to see Kovo glaring down at him with those red eyes. *Weakling*, said the crimson gaze. *Straggler*.

You're slowing us down.

You're holding us back.

Why should we try to save you?

You're already lost.

Conor wrenched his arm free and stumbled away from the ape and the hole, his back coming up against an outcropping. Pieces of wall flaked away behind him, revealing another small tunnel no wider than his hand, as if this section of the cave were a bad apple, riddled with wormholes.

And then, from somewhere deep inside the hole, he heard rustling.

At first he thought it was only the whispers in his head, but those were quiet and even. This sound was getting closer. Louder. A moment later Xanthe spun back, pink eyes narrowed, and Conor knew that she heard it, too.

"Get in the center of the cave," she whispered urgently.

Meilin was the first to move, putting her back to Xanthe and shifting fluidly into a warrior's stance, torchlight in one hand, quarterstaff in the other.

"What's going on?" asked Takoda, even as he and Kovo joined the circle.

"Is it the Many?" asked Conor, pushing off the wall and putting his back to Takoda's, the image of Phos Astos being overrun surging to mind. A tangle of pale bodies, empty eyes, clawing fingers.

Briggan crouched beside him, ready to lunge.

"No," said Xanthe, clutching her pack. "It's not the Many."

"Well, that's good," said Takoda. And then, in the ensuing silence, "Isn't that good, Xanthe?"

But the girl said nothing. The rustling sound grew nearer, the cave trembling and bits of stone crumbling away to reveal more and more holes, so many Conor thought the tunnel would collapse around them.

And then, embedded in the darkness, he saw the stars.

Conor's first thought was that they were somehow back above ground, that the cave had crumbled around them and revealed the night sky overhead. A brief rush of relief went through him. But then the stars began to blink and shift, and Conor realized with horror that they weren't stars at all, but *eyes*.

Dozens—no, hundreds—of milky white eyes.

Kovo growled, a sound deep in his chest, and Briggan bared his teeth. Conor waited for faces to form around the eyes, for the shapes of the creatures—whatever they were—to materialize, but they didn't. Instead, the eyes hovered, as if they belonged to the darkness itself. And then the darkness itself began to *move*.

"What on earth . . ." whispered Meilin.

"It's a cyrix nest!" said Xanthe, as if anyone but her knew what that meant. But the tone of her voice was enough to tell Conor that whatever a cyrix nest was, it was *bad*.

The darkness was alive with the creatures. The shadows and eyes shuddered forward together, pouring through the holes and into the cavern, writhing and coiling and blinking their hundred white pupils.

Meilin shouted, and brought her quarterstaff down on a tendril of darkness.

Xanthe took the torchlight and swung it into the writhing dark. The cyrix retreated from the fire just like actual shadows, but then a limb surged forward and struck Xanthe in the chest. The force sent her staggering back into Meilin. The torch fell from her grip and skittered away.

On the damp cave floor, the torchlight began to sputter and die.

In its faltering flame, Conor saw Kovo bring a massive fist down on a writhing shape, blocking out several white eyes as his hand connected with something both solid and insubstantial. The creature bent like jelly around the beast's blow. The force of the ape's attack shuddered through the darkness, and Conor realized with sick certainty that the seething shadows were *connected*.

The cyrix wasn't many things.

It was *one*.

One massive creature, either coming together or spreading apart, surrounding them in shadow and eyes and—somewhere, given their luck—teeth.

Something brushed against Conor's leg, and he tried to pull back, but the thing was already wrapping a smoky black tendril around his ankle. No, not a tendril. A *tentacle*. It latched on to him, cold seeping through his leg where the creature's touch met his skin. Conor gasped at the icy contact and tried to tear free, but the cyrix's grip only tightened. He felt himself losing ground, being dragged forward toward the nearest hole.

Conor stumbled and went down, grasping at the chalky floor for something, anything to hold on to as the cyrix pulled him toward the dark. A cry escaped his lips, and then he heard a growl and felt rushing air as a blur of fur tore past him. An instant later Briggan's teeth closed around the tentacle, and the wolf shook his head viciously, the way Conor had seen terriers do with rats.

The eye-dotted limb twitched in Briggan's mouth, and then wrenched itself free from the wolf's teeth and the boy's leg at the same time. It snaked down into the hole and out of sight.

But there were so many more.

Leg still tingling with cold, Conor grabbed a loose rock from the ground and hurled it at the nearest pair of eyes. The tentacle flinched back and then reared up to strike again as the torchlight faltered, plunging the cave into stuttering seconds of dark.

In the spasms of light, Conor saw Meilin swinging her quarterstaff, the motions fluid but wild, as if she didn't know where to strike; saw Xanthe digging through her pack, searching desperately for something; saw Kovo trying to put himself between Takoda and the monster, but the monster was *everywhere*!

"Does this thing have a weakness?" asked Conor, crouching to grab another rock.

"Yeah, Xanthe," snapped Meilin, lashing out at nothing. "How are we supposed to fight this thing?"

Just before the torchlight failed for good, Conor saw Xanthe pull something small and spherical from the pack.

"You don't fight a cyrix," she said, holding the sphere over her head. "You *run*."

The torchlight vanished, plunging them all into darkness, but Conor still squeezed his eyes shut. He knew what was coming, and an instant later Xanthe's hand must have tightened on the sphere, because light *exploded* through the cave. The cyrix hissed and recoiled, hundreds of star-like eyes vanishing like candles blown out by a gust. Xanthe wasted no time. She burst into movement, looking less like a girl and more like a ball of blue-white light as she ran for the nearest tunnel.

They all followed, ape and boys and girl and wolf, knowing that the flare would only buy them a few moments. But it was long enough. It had to be.

Conor was the last one out. He saw the extinguished torchlight and snatched it up, stumbling to keep up with the strange blaze of blue-white light ahead and not get left behind in shadow.

They ran when the path was even, and slid when the earth beneath them slanted away. They nearly collided with each other several times until the tunnel finally opened up, not into another cave, but into a massive cavern with half a dozen branching tunnels.

The ceiling rippled overhead. At the center of the cavern, pools of water shone like glass, emitting a faint greenish light.

Which was good, because the sphere in Xanthe's hand had petered out.

"Well . . ." Xanthe slowed and stopped, letting the spent flare tumble to the damp cavern floor. "That was my last light."

"Who knows," said Meilin, who barely looked winded. "Maybe we won't need any more."

Takoda let out a small, nervous laugh. He was leaning against Kovo's broad side. "Maybe," he said.

Conor had his hands on his knees, gasping for air, his head swimming with the chase. Briggan stood beside him, hackles still raised. Kovo's red eyes were trained on the darkness behind them, as if daring the cyrix to follow. But long moments passed, and no milky eyes swam in the shadows, no tendrils of darkness crept toward them.

"Are we safe?" asked Conor.

Xanthe squinted around, trying to get her bearings. She nodded and said, "For now."

Conor straightened and tried to manage a smile, but the world spun, and the horrible, squirming feeling under his skin redoubled. He clutched the crux of his arm, darkness swimming in his vision.

"Conor?" came Meilin's voice, too far away. "Are you okay?"

Okay, okay, okay, it echoed through the cavern and in his head, mixing with whispers.

Conor closed his eyes, opened them, swallowed.

"Yeah," he said, forcing himself to straighten. "Let's keep going." His eyes tracked to Xanthe, who stood reflected by a shallow pool, doubling into two, four, many. She turned toward him, her pink eyes multiplied.

"Are you sure?" she asked. "You look sick."

Sick, sick, sick.

Conor looked to Meilin, who shook her head. Xanthe didn't know, not about the parasite crawling through him, infecting him the way it had so many of her people. He tried to find the words but Meilin answered first.

"He's tired," she said. "We all are."

Conor managed a nod, but Xanthe's gaze lingered, eyes narrowing. "I'm okay," he said shakily. To prove it, he took a step, and then another. "We need to keep moving."

"Okay," said Takoda, looking around at the cavern with its many branching tunnels. "Where do we go from here?"

UNWELCOME NEWS

THE LOW BRANCH CREAKED BENEATH ABEKE'S FEET.

She moved carefully across the tree limbs, watching, listening, an arrow already nocked in her bow, but the only sounds that met her ears were the sounds of any forest, the rustle of leaves and the trill of birds and the shuffle of small creatures in the branches and the brush. Somewhere on the ground below, Uraza prowled, and overhead, Rollan's gyrfalcon, Essix, was a shadow against the clouds, circling soundlessly.

Abeke shouldered the bow and climbed higher, until she broke through the forest canopy. In the distance, she could see the water that separated Amaya from Greenhaven, the dark shape of boats. They were almost to the water. Slowly, she descended back into the trees. Her body still ached from the fight with Zerif and his stolen beasts— *How?* How had he taken so many? And the even scarier question, *Why?*—and a deeper pain ran through her from whatever had shaken her own bond with Uraza. The first was muscle and bone. The second was something worse. Something that *scared* her.

They needed to get back to the Greencloaks' fortress.

Olvan would know what was happening, what to do. She hoped.

Beneath her, Uraza's dark shape slid past.

And then, all of a sudden, the leopard stopped.

Her head sank low and her tail flicked, nose twitching as if scenting prey.

Or predator.

Abeke held her breath and nocked an arrow in her bow, her mind spiraling through a dozen possible threats. Had Zerif come back? Had one of his infected animals stayed behind? What was lurking in the woods?

The big cat crouched, hesitated, and then pounced.

An instant later, a tinny shriek, cut short by Uraza's strong jaws, and the leopard reappeared, a limp woodland creature in her mouth.

Abeke rolled her eyes as the cat looked up at her, as if offering to share.

"That's okay," she whispered. "You can keep it."

Uraza blinked her violet eyes and began to play with her snack, and Abeke straightened and made her way back across the branches to the clearing where they'd camped. It was little more than a few trampled strides of treeless earth near the edge of the woods. Two exhausted figures huddled around a small fire contained by a circle of rocks.

She dropped to the forest floor, the mossy earth cushioning the force and sound of her landing.

"No sign of Zerif," she said.

Rollan jumped like a startled cat and spun, gripping the tiny stick he'd been using to nudge the fire. Its end smoked faintly. When he saw Abeke, he slumped back onto the dead log he'd been using as a seat. "Way to give a guy a heart attack," he said, tossing the stick back into the fire. "I didn't hear you coming."

"Sorry." Abeke managed a tired smile. "That's kind of the idea."

Rollan rolled his head on his shoulders. Abeke's attention went to the other figure, a boy in animal skins and a woven grass belt, his back against a fallen tree, a livid bruise against his cheek. Abeke's chest tightened. Anda. The boy had left his family, his tribe, and they hadn't been able to keep him safe. Where he had looked lean before, now he looked fragile, his narrow form gone gaunt from the wound at his side and the loss of Tellun.

Abeke didn't know what it felt like to lose a spirit animal, but she could see the pain in his eyes. Supposedly it was like losing a loved one, or a limb, a piece of yourself. Abeke made a silent promise that she and Rollan and Meilin and Conor would find a way to stop Zerif, heal the Evertree, and return Anda's spirit animal.

When she thought about the tasks, they felt impossible. But Abeke reminded herself of all the impossible things they'd already done. They could handle a few more.

Still, she had to admit that the three of them had looked better.

They wouldn't have escaped Zerif at all, not without the help of the figure in the red cloak. Who was he? How was he strong enough to face a Great Beast? And why had he helped them? Abeke had so many questions for the stranger, but of course, he wasn't there to answer. He'd vanished into the trees after Zerif. It had taken all Abeke's restraint not to hunt the man down herself, but Anda needed her, and so did Rollan. They had to stick together, had to deliver Anda to Greenhaven, even without his spirit animal, Tellun.

Abeke shuddered at the thought of Uraza being taken from her. Even though she'd only had Uraza for a relatively short time, she couldn't remember what it felt like to live without her. Just the thought of it made her ill, an echo of the sickness she'd felt when the earth had shaken and her bond with the leopard had felt stretched to breaking. Those strange tremors were bad enough, and left her feeling like the earth and everything in it was being pulled and torn . . . but to lose Uraza entirely?

How? How could a person be separated from their spirit animal? How could Anda bear it?

But of course, he wasn't bearing it, not well. His skin looked sallow, and his arms were pressed around his wounded side, where Suka the Polar Bear had slashed him. But she could tell the severed bond hurt him even more. There was nothing she could do for that, but his other injuries still needed tending.

Abeke crouched in front of the boy and dug some berries from her pocket. She'd found a high-growing bush in the forest, their seeds known to help with pain. Anda took them without question, his eyes never leaving the ground, where several elk tracks marked the last sign of his spirit animal.

"It's not far to the water," said Abeke. "We'll be back at Greenhaven soon."

"What's the point?" whispered Anda, so softly she almost didn't hear.

"You're still one of us," said Abeke, but Anda only shrugged, defeated.

Rollan said nothing. He had tipped his head back, eyes closed. She recognized the blankness in his face and knew he was looking through Essix's eyes, seeing for himself what she had seen above the canopy. A few moments later he blinked, gaze returning to Abeke and Anda and the dying fire. He nodded and helped the other boy to his feet. Anda leaned heavily against Rollan, beads of sweat running down his face and staining the skins that wrapped around his shoulder.

Uraza appeared at the edge of the small clearing and began to pace, wearing paths into the forest floor. Abeke knew the leopard preferred to roam freely, but she'd stand out too much in the clearing leading down to the shore, and she wasn't a fan of the crossing to Greenhaven. Besides, what had Zerif said to Anda before he stole the Great Beast?

That he hadn't learned to bring Tellun into the passive state. If the elk had been in its passive state, would it have been safe?

"Uraza?" called Abeke, holding out her hand, a gesture the leopard knew well. But Uraza did not come. The Great Beast's violet eyes shone with a wild glint, her tail flicking nervously. Panic wound through Abeke's chest.

"Uraza," she said, forcing strength and certainty into her voice.

The leopard slunk several paces, head low beneath her shoulders, looking less like a spirit animal than a predator.

"Please," said Abeke softly.

The big cat stopped pacing, and seemed to *see* Abeke

for the first time. Her head lifted, as if catching a scent, and her mouth lolled open as she padded forward, soft dark fur brushing Abeke's hand before Uraza vanished in a flash of light. A sudden heat flared against Abeke's skin, and then the mark was there on her arm where it should be.

She touched her fingers to it, trying to draw comfort.

And yet . . . she could still feel the distance, the invisible cord between them drawing taut and slack and taut again, its strength uncertain. How long would it hold?

"Abeke?" She dragged her attention up and saw Rollan, shifting his weight as he tried to support Anda. "Are you ready?"

She nodded, and the three made their way out of the forest and toward the water in silence.

"Stew. A bath. Stew. A real bed." Rollan helped drag the boat up onto the shore.

He had decided to pass the journey across the water by listing everything he planned to enjoy once they were back. Even though Abeke knew the only thing Rollan really cared about finding there was Meilin. Well, maybe Meilin and stew.

"Wait, did I already say stew?"

"I'm pretty sure you mentioned it," said Abeke, tying off the rope. She looked around, but the docks were strangely empty. Up ahead, Greenhaven loomed.

Rollan's mood seemed to brighten with every step toward the gates, but the closer they drew, the more Abeke had a gnawing sense that *something* was wrong.

It wasn't anything specific, just a gut sense, but years of tracking and hunting in Nilo had taught her to pay attention when that feeling in her chest flared in warning. Surely if Abeke and Rollan had felt the strain on their bonds, the other Greencloaks had, too. Hopefully they knew what was happening, and how to stop it.

"Hey," said Rollan, trying to hide his interest as they climbed the steps to the gate. "Conor and Meilin, they have to be back by now, right?"

Abeke smiled. "I'm sure. After all, they were only going to investigate the door in the Petral Mountains."

"Let's hope they ran into less trouble than we did." His voice was light when he said it, but something twinged in Abeke's stomach.

"Yeah," she said quietly. "Let's hope."

By the time they passed through the gate and into the courtyard, Abeke could feel the tension in the air. Every face she saw seemed drawn, and the guards all had their weapons out, their postures tense, as if they were trying to hold their ground against a wind.

But it wasn't just what Abeke *saw* that gave her pause, but what she *didn't* see. Something was missing.

And then Abeke realized, it was the spirit animals.

Every time she'd been to Greenhaven, she'd been met with parrots and foxes, meerkats and pelicans, a hedgehog and a boa constrictor and a dozen other beasts. They dotted the fortress with color, filled the air with sound. But now they were gone—no, not gone, of course, just drawn into their passive states. The black tattoos stuck out from collars and cuffs. Whatever had happened to Rollan and Abeke back in the Amayan forest, it had obviously happened here at Greenhaven, too. And the Greencloaks must be just as scared.

Only two animals were in sight: Olvan's moose, standing sentry at the edge of the courtyard, and Essix, still circling overhead. She was an ornery bird, as stubborn as Rollan.

But where was Kovo? The last time she'd been here, the Great Ape had been in the center of the square, surrounded by guards. Even as a spirit animal, he took up space. But there was no sign of him. Or Jhi. Or Briggan.

Rollan eased Anda down onto the steps outside the great hall. A medic rushed forward to see to the boy's wounds. He didn't resist, didn't even speak, only let the woman lead him away. Abeke caught him as he passed and squeezed his shoulder once, gently.

"It's going to be okay," she said.

Anda nodded vaguely but said nothing. The sadness in his eyes broke Abeke's heart.

"Some welcome party," said Rollan, turning in a circle. "Meilin?" he called out. "Conor?"

"I'm afraid they are not here," said Olvan, the leader of the Greencloaks, appearing at the entrance of the great hall. He looked older, or perhaps just tired, new creases etched into his face.

"Shouldn't they be back by now?" asked Rollan, fear edging his voice. "You . . . you went with them."

"Yes," said Olvan slowly. "I did."

"Then where are they?" demanded Rollan.

"What's going on?" asked Abeke, heart racing.

Olvan hesitated, his wrinkles deepening in thought. His eyes tracked over the courtyard, as if he didn't want to speak of what had happened, not even in front of his own Greencloaks. Abeke's chest tightened, the way it did when she was on uneven ground and could feel it shifting, about to give way.

What had happened to her friends?

When Olvan spoke again, his voice was carefully even, but his gaze was filled with warning. "You two look as though you've had your own troubles," he said, holding open the door to the great hall. "Come inside, and we can compare notes."

"What do you mean, they're *trapped*?"

"Lower your voice, Rollan," instructed Olvan. The boy's words still echoed through the great hall.

Trapped . . . trapped . . . trapped.

Abeke looked around then, and realized that the great hall, usually buzzing with activity, had been emptied. The three of them were alone, Abeke and Rollan on one side of the long wooden table, and Olvan on the other. The surface of the table was piled with scrolls, and bowls of stew waited in front of them, quickly cooling as they sat untouched, forgotten.

"We don't know exactly what happened," explained Olvan, "only that the doorway collapsed behind them."

"*What?*" squawked Rollan.

Abeke listened but said nothing. She ran her finger-tips along the table's surface, considering the hundreds of marks—scratches, dents, grooves—in its surface, focusing on the details as she tried to organize her thoughts.

She worried about them all, but she worried about Conor most. He was running out of time, and she couldn't stop thinking about the mark crawling up his arm, about what would happen when—if—it reached his forehead.

The fight with Zerif came back to her, the horrible spiral on his face. The same mark was echoed in every one of the animals he now controlled, and the thought of him controlling Conor, too, made her stomach turn.

"You didn't want to tell us in the open," she said slowly. "The other Greencloaks don't know, do they?"

Olvan rubbed his eyes. "Not all of them, no."

Rollan looked pale with anger. "Why on Erdas not?"

The old man sighed. "The last few weeks have been trying on all of us, mentally as well as physically. I fear that this turn of events would be a blow we cannot afford."

"I don't care about the Greencloaks' morale," snapped Rollan. "Not when our *friends* are stuck under the earth with *Kovo*, the ape who tried to destroy the world!"

Abeke reached out and brought a hand to Rollan's arm. She could feel his body, as tense as rope, beneath his cloak.

Olvan, for his part, looked as if he were carrying the weight of Erdas on his shoulders. Abeke could tell it was taking all his strength to keep his own voice even, his manner calm.

"Kovo is not what he once was," said Olvan steadily.

"Look," said Rollan, "I'm all about redemption, but you'll never make me believe that Kovo is on our side."

"He is on *Takoda's* side," offered Abeke, "and Takoda is on ours."

"Takoda is trapped under the ground with the rest of our friends!" shouted Rollan, pushing to his feet. "How can you just sit there listening to this, Abeke? We have to go after them!"

"Sit," commanded Olvan. "Where they've gone, you can't follow. The door has caved in, and it's too fragile to force our way through. Your friends are still alive—"

"How do you know?" Abeke cut in.

Olvan gestured at the mountain of scrolls on the wooden table, ribbons of red and blue and yellow tying them shut. "Word comes from many sources, Lenori among them. She can feel Briggan and Jhi, as well as Kovo. They are all still alive."

"That doesn't mean they're safe!" protested Rollan.

"Have faith in your friends," said Olvan. "*I* do. And know that you are needed here. With Zerif infecting people and stealing spirit animals, it's more important than ever that you two find the Great Beasts before he does. Bring them here to Greenhaven so that we can protect them from whatever he's planning."

"But we failed," said Abeke, her throat tightening. "Anda lost Tellun."

Olvan's eyes darkened. Abeke could see the worry in his expression. Not only for Anda, but for all of them, for whatever Zerif was planning, whatever he would do when—*if*—he got the rest of the Great Beasts. "Tell me everything."

Abeke swallowed hard, and explained what had happened—first with Anda's tribe, and then the appearance of Zerif and his stolen Great Beasts, the loss of the elk, the horrible strain on their spirit animal bonds.

"We, too, felt the straining of our bonds," said Olvan grimly. "We can only assume it's because of the Evertree's rot. Lenori tells us that her own bond shuddered when the tree did."

"And then there was the guy in the mask," said Rollan, stabbing a spoon at his now-cold stew.

At this, Olvan stilled. "What guy?"

"He showed up at the last minute," said Abeke thoughtfully. "He's the only reason we got away."

"He had a red cloak," offered Rollan, "and he wore some kind of mask. Weird and faceless, gave me the creeps. Didn't say anything. But Abeke's right, he did help us."

"The way he fought . . ." said Abeke.

"It was insane," said Rollan, spirits brightening a little despite himself.

"I've never seen anything like it," added Abeke. "Not from Meilin, or my people, or even Zerif. It was like he . . . wasn't human. It was as if a spirit animal were giving him strength, but there was no animal around. Not that I saw."

Olvan steepled his fingers. "Strange. A similar figure appeared here at Greenhaven not long ago, but his mask had the face of an animal carved in it. Some kind of cat."

"So there's more of them?" asked Rollan.

"It would appear so. This one called himself Worthy. He came asking for the Keeper. They left together and haven't returned. For now, we must treat these strangers with caution. We don't know if they are friends or foes."

"But the one in the woods," insisted Abeke, "he *helped* us."

"Yet he conceals his face," countered the leader of the Greencloaks. "We may share a common enemy in Zerif. But if you cross paths with him again, be careful."

Rollan slumped back in his seat. "So, what now?" he grumbled. "We're just supposed to sit here, waiting for news of our friends? Waiting for Zerif to strike again? Waiting for the Evertree's rot to break our spirit animal bonds?"

"No." Olvan shook his head. "I don't expect you to sit here, waiting for anything." He began sorting through the pile of scrolls on the table, searching for one in particular. Some were large, obviously brought by hand, while others were small and tightly coiled, the kind carried by messenger birds. Each was bound with a ribbon, yellow or red or blue . . . never green. Abeke wondered if that would be too obvious. A message just asking to fall into the wrong hands.

Finally Olvan found the one he was looking for and plucked it out of the stack.

"This just arrived from Lenori." He slid the yellow tie from the paper and unrolled it. "Another Great Beast has awoken. So eat up and get your rest, because you two leave at first light."

"What about Anda?" asked Abeke.

Olvan sighed. "As soon as he's strong enough, we'll return him to Amaya and help him find his tribe."

Abeke bristled at the idea that the boy was useless without Tellun. "But he belongs with—"

The man reached out and curled his old hand over hers. "It's not your fault, but Anda has no place here without his Great Beast."

A new wave of guilt rolled over her. They'd taken him away, all for nothing. The only thing she could do now was fight for him. For Tellun.

Rollan sat forward on the bench.

"So where are we going?" he asked.

Olvan pinned down the scroll with his mug and finally met their eyes.

"You're going," he said, "to Stetriol."

SETTING SAIL

EVERYONE HAD OBVIOUSLY LOST THEIR MINDS.

That was the only explanation Rollan could come up with.

He shook his head and spit over the edge of the battlements. It was the middle of the night, the wind biting at his cheeks and messing his hair. He couldn't quiet his thoughts enough to sleep.

Stetriol, of all places. It couldn't have been Nilo, or Eura, or Amaya, or Zhong, or even Arctica! It had to be *Stetriol*.

He would rather face everyone he'd ever stolen from than set foot back in the land of the Conquerors and the Bile, Gerathon and Gar, the Reptile King and Shane.

Olvan claimed that the land at the edge of the world was different now, that it had changed. According to the leader of the Greencloaks, Stetriol was now full of happy people and frolicking pets and rainbows and—fine, Rollan might be exaggerating.

But still.

The last time he'd been in Stetriol, they'd tried to kill him. In fact, every encounter Rollan had had with Stetriol and its people had been *unpleasant*. And no matter what Olvan said, Rollan wasn't suddenly ready to assume the best from people who'd once showed him the worst.

"They're rebuilding," Olvan had insisted. "And we are helping them. We must show them they can trust us."

Rollan fought back a snort at that. Trust. He hadn't survived the streets of Concorba by trusting the people who were nice to him, let alone the ones who tried to stab him in the back. Sure, Stetriol had been through some bad times, but it had been cut off from the world for a *reason*.

"Stetriol is now a post, occupied by Greencloaks," Olvan had explained. "Our presence there is as large as it is here in Greenhaven, so you'll be in good hands once you arrive. And this time you won't be traveling alone."

In the end, those words had helped to ease Rollan's nerves a little. But he still wished Meilin was going with him. Wished she were *here*. He knew she'd had to go with Conor, so Jhi could help heal him, but it didn't change the fact that Rollan *missed* her. Not that he'd say that to her face. She'd probably just tease him if he did.

Or maybe she wouldn't.

Girls were confusing.

The wind on the battlements picked up. Rollan pulled his cloak tight around his shoulders. Below, the ocean made a constant shushing sound against the shore, while overhead it was a cloudless night with a bright wedge of a moon and a sea of stars. The kind of night that made Rollan feel small, though not in a bad way. Like he was part of something bigger.

He picked at the edge of his green cloak, the garment he'd been so hesitant to put on. After all, being alone could be scary, but being a part of something was way scarier. And yet, being a part of the Greencloaks had helped him get his own mother back, had brought him close to Abeke, Conor, and Meilin. It had given him family, friends, things he thought he'd never have.

He felt like he'd stolen something precious, and gotten away with it.

Rollan forced himself to smile. Once a thief, always a thief.

But someone—Zerif—was trying to steal those things back, and Rollan wasn't letting go without a fight. He took a long, steadying breath and was about to whistle for Essix when he heard the footsteps behind him. Not the march of boots down in the courtyard, but the soft familiar shuffle of Abeke's steps somewhere at his back. Rollan didn't turn around. He knew that if he heard her coming, it was only because she *wanted* him to hear. He'd never met anyone so stealthy.

Meilin the warrior. Abeke the tracker. Conor the loyal leader.

What did that make him?

"Can't sleep?" asked Abeke, emerging from the shadow of the keep wall.

Rollan shook his head.

"Essix is restless," he said, blaming the bird. The falcon appeared for an instant against the moon, then was gone again, swallowed up by the sky.

"I can't sleep either," said Abeke. "Every time I close my eyes, I'm afraid I'll wake to that feeling. . . ."

Rollan knew the feeling she was talking about. He'd felt it, too. Like his skeleton was being torn from his body with the skin still on. Like something important inside of him was bending, bending, about to break.

"It seems like you and Essix are okay."

"Me and Essix . . ." said Rollan, squinting up at the night sky. Was that true? "We've always let each other be. If this spirit animal bond is like a rope, maybe there's just more slack in ours. I mean, remember how long it took me to convince Essix to even go into her passive state?" Rollan took up a loose pebble and lobbed it over the wall. "Silly bird."

He tried to keep his voice steady, but the truth was, Rollan was scared. He was having a harder time borrowing Essix's sight these days. Even when he did, it felt unsteady, like he might fall at any second. Every time, he was left feeling dizzy, and like he'd eaten something rotten.

Rollan forced himself to take a deep breath. He felt trapped.

Trapped, like Meilin and Conor.

"Do you think they're okay, Abeke?" He didn't have to say who.

Abeke eased up beside him and leaned on the battlement. "Meilin's a warrior. And Conor . . . he's a fighter. The only way for us to help them is to stop Zerif. And to do that, we have to get to Stetriol before he does."

"Stetriol," grumbled Rollan. "Land of the Conquerors, and Shane, and all the people who hate us."

Abeke touched his shoulder. "People change," she said. "Look at us. None of us are the same people we were when this first started. Whoever thought you'd finally put on that green cloak?"

Rollan snorted.

"Besides, abandoning Stetriol is what got the Greencloaks into trouble last time." She looked out at the night. "You, me, Meilin, Conor, we're supposed to be the future of the Greencloaks. If we choose not to help, we're just repeating the past. We have to be better . . . okay?"

"Okay." Rollan bumped into her shoulder. "When did you get to be so smart?" he asked. "Are you hiding a talisman or something? Which Great Beast had all the brains?"

"Ha-ha."

"We should get you some mystic robes. You can go around telling futures or advising nobles or whatever people in mystic robes do . . ." He trailed off into a yawn, and Abeke broke into a smile.

"Come on," she said, steering him toward the stairwell. "We both need sleep if we're going to set out at first light." She cast a last glance back at the night, the moon, the glittering water. "Something tells me we're going to need our strength."

"Hoist!"

"Bartel, hand up that crate."

"Careful with the apples."

"Gera, got your medical bag below."

"Have you checked the sail lines?"

"Don't let those blades get wet!"

The sun was barely up, and the Greenhaven dock was already a flurry of activity. Rollan had secretly hoped that "we sail at first light" actually meant "we sail at a perfectly decent hour sometime after breakfast," but his hopes had been dashed when Olvan pounded on his door before dawn.

"I'm up, I'm up," he'd mumbled before rolling over and trying to stifle the beginning of dawn's light with his pillow. But when he tried to close his eyes again he'd seen Meilin clawing through the dark, and Zerif's grim smile, and the wormy black spiral forcing itself across Tellun's forehead, and he knew that sleep was ruined.

Now, as they made their way to the shore, Abeke looked almost as tired as he felt, and far less excited about the ship waiting for them at the end of the docks.

While she'd grown more comfortable with boats over time, Abeke had always preferred being on land. Plus, Uraza got seasick. The short trip from the Amayan coast was one thing, but a sea voyage to Stetriol was another.

Rollan's spirits were considerably brighter. Growing up on the streets of Concorba, he'd dreamed of fresh air and freedom, and life aboard a ship afforded both. Besides, when it came to modes of transportation, sailing was about as far from riding a horse as he could get, and in Rollan's book, that was a mark in its favor.

The *Tellun's Pride II* was a beautiful craft, sturdy with brilliant white sails, but it wasn't the ship that caught Rollan's attention: It was the crew!

Not a handful of escorts, but a *proper* crew of fifteen—no, twenty!—Greencloaks. All for their mission to Stetriol. The sight of them made Rollan feel rather important.

"This is quite an expedition," said Abeke. "Will we draw too much attention?"

Rollan deflated a little. Of course, she was the one to think of stealth.

"I've sent word ahead," answered Olvan. "They know you're coming. Besides, half of these Greencloaks are going to relieve those who are already stationed there."

Rollan deflated a little more. And then Abeke knocked his shoulder with hers and flashed him a smile, and he felt himself smile back. It was still an impressive crew. And besides, they were the chosen ones! They'd gone on their last quest without any help at all! And, okay, maybe that was a bad example because it didn't end so well, but still . . .

"Awfully small for Greencloaks, aren't they?" said a voice behind them.

Rollan and Abeke turned to find two figures in forest green ambling down the docks toward them, packs on their shoulders. The first was a woman, tall with warm dark skin, a shock of short black hair, and silver in her ears. The second was a man, a head shorter and stockier, with pale hair pulled back in a ponytail.

"I was beginning to wonder if you'd join us!" said Olvan.

"Sorry we're late," said the woman. Her voice had a slight Niloan cadence.

"S'my fault," said the man, who was all Eura. His collar was open beneath his cloak, and across the skin of his chest Rollan could see the edge of a tattoo. It looked like a monkey. Or at least a monkey's tail.

"Of course it's your fault," said the woman, but her tone was cheerful. "Just be glad they didn't sail without us."

Her sleeves were rolled up, revealing a parrot tattoo that ran the length of her forearm, from talons to crest. She leaned her elbow on the man's shoulder, and he didn't seem to mind. In fact, he leaned into her as if they were old friends.

Will Abeke and I be like that one day? Rollan wondered. It was easy to imagine staying friends, but it was hard to picture getting so . . . *old.*

"That would be hard to do," said Olvan, "considering you're the captain."

Rollan's eyes widened in surprise, but Abeke broke into a grin.

"Which makes me the first mate," said the man. "And you two must be our cargo."

"I'm nobody's cargo!" said Rollan, at the same time Abeke said, *"Cargo?"*

He only chuckled.

"I'm Nisha," said the woman, "and this is—"

"Oi, I can introduce myself," cut in the man. "Arac. I'm Arac."

Nisha raised a brow, obviously amused. "Do you feel better now?"

"Much," grunted Arac. "A name's a powerful thing to have," he said, addressing Abeke and Rollan. "Can't go handing it off to anyone."

"I'm not anyone, *Arac*, I'm your wife."

Rollan's mouth fell open. He'd never met married Greencloaks before. Now he could see why.

"Close your mouth, boy," warned Nisha. "Before something flies in."

Abeke giggled as Rollan's mouth snapped shut.

"Chop-chop," said Nisha, striding up the plank.

"You heard the woman—er, I mean captain," Arac amended when she cut him a glance. In a fluid gesture he took up Rollan's and Abeke's sacks and hoisted them onto one strong shoulder.

"You can see I'm leaving you in good hands," said Olvan.

Abeke shot the elder Greencloak a worried look. To Rollan's surprise, the lightness left the old man's face and he knelt, resting a hand on each of their shoulders.

"Any advice?" asked Rollan.

"Yes. Take care. Watch out. And come back safe."

"That's awfully general," said Rollan, tipping his head. "You got anything more specific?"

Olvan swallowed. "If you see that stranger, the one with the mask and the red cloak, be careful." Olvan straightened, his joints popping and cracking with the effort. "I'm counting on you two," he said. "We all are."

"No pressure," grumbled Rollan as Olvan mounted his spirit animal and made his way back up toward Greenhaven's keep. Rollan thought he could see Anda beside the gate, dark eyes wide and watching. Rollan lifted a hand, but the boy—if it was him—didn't respond.

"Get aboard or get left," called Arac, pounding a meaty fist along the ship's hull.

Abeke and Rollan climbed the ramp, and both cast a last glance back at Greenhaven as the ship put out to sea. They stood there watching as the fortress shrank and shrank, until it was lost from sight.

"Off on another adventure," said Abeke, leaning back against a crate.

"I wonder if Stetriol has good stew," said Rollan. Abeke touched her stomach as if the thought were unwelcome, and closed her eyes.

Overhead, Essix let out a short cry and swooped down toward the deck.

"I was wondering when you'd show up," he said, trying not to sound relieved.

Essix landed on the ship's rail just long enough to claim a scratch under her beak and another between her wings. Then she was off again, and so were they.

CALL TO THE KING

THE BOY SAT ON A LOW ROCK, SHARPENING A PAIR OF knives.

He was perched in the shadow of the tree line, shielded by a canopy of leaves while he worked. His cloak, a vivid red, sat at his feet, folded inside out to hide the crimson. His sleeves, crisp and black but torn from the fight with Zerif, were rolled to his elbows. The only sound beside the sh-sh of stone against metal was the rustling of branches overhead, their leaves caught up by the breeze. Now and then, his lips formed words—as if he were talking to himself, or to someone else, or simply remembering conversations long past—but they never took shape, never found sound.

His mask, a smooth plane of white wood, sat cast aside him on the stone. Unlike the others, with their ears and snouts, their horns and tusks, his mask held no such markings. It was even, featureless, save for the slits through which he saw and breathed and spoke.

When the knives were clean and sharp, he set them aside and rolled his head on his shoulders, trying to work out the stiffness that had settled in his muscles. A cut ran along his jaw—it was a testament to the force of the blow, that it even broke the skin—and his muscles ached, but he was alive, and so were the Greencloaks. But he hadn't been fast enough to save Tellun.

And in the end, Zerif had gotten away with his newest prize, vanishing in the trees.

The man seemed at times a monster, at others a ghost.

In the distance, the sun sank over the water, turning the ocean and the sky from blue to orange and purple and gold, the colors of a fading bruise. A clearing stretched between the boy's perch at the edge of the woods and the shore, and the boat waiting for him on the docks.

As soon as night fell, he would go.

Until then, he tended his weapons and nursed his shallow wounds. As he dabbed fresh salve over the cuts, his skin caught the setting sun, illuminating the band of scales that tapered down his forearm like armor, shifting from green to gold.

He paused, arm outstretched before him, and stared at the scales, marveling now the way he had when he'd first seen them. When he flexed his arm, they shifted in response, not like well-fit clothing, but like skin itself. He lifted a fingernail and ran it thoughtfully along their plated surface.

A bird screeched overhead.

Not a falcon or a pigeon, but a *crow*, a Ksenian crow, a southern tracking bird with a dash of white on its forehead. He held out his scaled arm, and the bird landed on his wrist. A message was bound to its leg with a single piece of dark red cloth.

The message was from Stead.

He recognized the young man's short, blocky script, even before he read the note.

Only a few lines, but that was all he needed.

King, it read.

A Great Beast has risen.

Return to Stetriol.

He jostled his arm, and the bird hopped free, waiting with curious eyes while the boy dug a piece of charred wood from his pocket, turned the scrap of paper over on the stone, and scribbled an answer. He then retied the note to the crow's foot. It clicked its beak, clearly expecting a reward. He fed it a scrap of dried meat and sent it on its way. Within moments, the bird was a speck of black in the reddish glare of the setting sun, winging its way toward the sea, King's message bound to its foot.

A single line, signed with a *K*.

Already on my way.

The boy they called King squinted until the crow was lost from sight, then slid his knives back into their holsters and took up his mask. He fastened it over his face, settled the red cloak back on his shoulders, and made his way to the boat bobbing on the dock.

To Stetriol.

SHADOW PLAY

TUNNEL AND CAVERN.

   Tunnel and cavern.

Tunnel and cavern.

Meilin had been trained to map the terrain in her mind so she never got lost, but it didn't work down here. Not when everything looked the same! They were beneath the earth, she knew, but how far beneath? Feet? Miles? How long since the doorway had collapsed? How long had they been trapped underground, wandering the corridors of Sadre, the world under the soil? Days? Weeks? Time ran together just like the tunnels and caverns.

Meilin had tried to keep track, marking time on her sleeve with a bit of blackish chalk, but she'd given up one night after slipping in a puddle, the muddy water smudging the tallies beyond recognition.

Tunnel and cavern.

Tunnel and cavern.

It was maddening.

Down here, there was no up or down, no forward or back, no day or night. Time bled, and the simple beat of

Meilin's heart was deafening in her ears. She couldn't distract herself from worries about Abeke, and Rollan, and Conor. She reached for Jhi's calm, which usually came to her, even in the panda's passive form, but where it once wrapped around her, now it felt more like a grazing touch. Still, Meilin clung to that comfort and resisted the urge to scream.

"We should stop here," said Xanthe when their tunnel gave way to another cavern. "I'm sure we could all use some rest."

Meilin looked around. It looked like almost every other space they'd passed through.

"Is it night?" she asked, before remembering that outside of Phos Astos, Xanthe likely had no way to keep track of day and night. "I mean . . . is it the time when you normally sleep? How do you even measure the hours?"

This wasn't the first time Meilin had asked that question, but Xanthe still answered patiently. "By the sound of the water in the rocks, and how tall the ground blooms are, and whether or not the wall rushes are awake." Then she shrugged and added, "And how tired I am."

"I think it's fascinating," said Takoda. "I mean, what is day and night without the sun and moon? How does a body know the cycles of need?"

Kovo and Meilin rolled their eyes at the same time, then caught each other and glared. She didn't trust the ape or his scarlet gaze—a look that seemed constantly challenging, a body always on the verge of action. And yet what help had he been? He'd gotten them trapped here beneath the earth, and now he didn't seem to be doing anything but biding his time. *For what?*

Briggan gave a soft whimper, and Meilin turned to find Conor half walking, half stumbling, bracing himself against a handhold of rock.

"I also judge the time," said Xanthe soberly, "by how badly your friend needs to rest."

"I'm all right," mumbled Conor, but his blond hair was sticking to his face with sweat. Meilin could tell he was suffering. "I'm . . ." He trailed off as a shudder passed through him.

Meilin reached for his arm, but to her shock Conor jerked backward, a hiss escaping his throat.

The sound was so strange, so utterly *inhuman*, it stopped her in her tracks. Conor's hands curled, not all the way into fists, but claws, and his expression twisted into something animal, his eyes vacant, and his mouth half open in a snarl.

Briggan leaped forward and put himself between Conor and the rest, not to protect him, Meilin realized with a start, but to protect *them*. Kovo growled and wrapped his arms protectively around Takoda.

"What's going on?" demanded Xanthe, pink eyes wide. "What's wrong with him?"

Conor's chest heaved as Meilin inched forward. Xanthe tried to pull her back, but she held up a hand, her eyes trained on her friend.

"Conor," whispered Meilin. "You're stronger than this. Fight it."

The boy squeezed his eyes shut, another shiver rolling through him. Then he blinked and looked up, and his eyes widened. He was Conor again. The boy from Trunswick. The kindhearted Greencloak who'd stood beside her through thick and thin.

"Meilin," he whispered. "I'm . . . I'm sorry . . ."

He tried to take a step forward, but his knees buckled. Meilin was there by his side, catching him before he could fall. He was burning up as she lowered him to the cave floor, and when she pulled his shirt aside and saw the vicious curl of the parasite against his bicep, inching up toward his shoulder, his throat, his head.

Xanthe saw the mark then, and leaped away with a gasp. "He's *infected*."

"But he's fighting it," said Takoda.

Xanthe shook her head. "Do you honestly think we would have cast our own people out if they could be saved? There *is* no way to fight it."

"I refuse to believe that," snapped Meilin. "He's still my friend."

"Not for long," said Xanthe, wrapping her arms around herself. "And once the mark takes him, he'll be able to infect *us*. This is how one become many. He can't come with us, Meilin."

"I'm not leaving him behind," she said as she took the cloak from her shoulders, folding it for a pillow beneath Conor's head.

"I'm sorry, but there's no saving him."

"You don't know that," snapped Meilin. "If we get to the Wyrm, if we defeat it . . ." She could hear the desperation in her own voice; she knew how it sounded, but she wasn't just trying to make herself feel better. She believed he could be saved. She had to believe it. "Look, if he loses control, then . . ."

"Then what?"

"Then we'll talk," said Meilin. "But until then, he stays with us." She looked up. "Even if that means you won't."

Silence fell over them, broken only by Conor's fevered breathing. Xanthe's eyes flicked from Meilin to Takoda and Kovo, then down to Conor. The way she looked at him, like he was already gone, turned Meilin's stomach. She gripped Conor's shoulder. She knew what it felt like, to be trapped inside your skin, to be fighting against someone else's control. She knew the fear, and the helplessness, and the *hopelessness* of that fight, and she wouldn't let him go through it, not alone.

"Xanthe," she said, fighting to keep her voice even. "I don't know if we can do this without you, but I *won't* do this without Conor."

Xanthe's pink eyes met hers. "Okay," she said at last. "I'll stay."

"Thank you," whispered Meilin.

Xanthe tried to manage a smile. "You wouldn't make it far without me," she said, but Meilin could see the darker truth in Xanthe's pale eyes. The girl had nowhere else to go. No one to go *to*.

From the floor, Conor let out a small, stifled sound of pain, and Meilin flinched.

Jhi, she called desperately. With a flash of light and a quick burst of heat, the panda was there beside her in the cavern. Jhi's head swiveled slowly to get her bearings, obviously hoping to find herself back above ground.

Sorry, thought Meilin. *Not yet.*

The panda turned her steady gaze on Conor's prone form. Jhi's face remained passive, and where that lack of expression used to frustrate Meilin, now she clung to it, trying to absorb the panda's calm. Jhi leaned forward and rested a single paw on Conor's chest, while Briggan paced, his hackles still raised.

For a long moment, no one said anything.

And then Xanthe clapped her hands. "Like I was say-ing," she said, an edge of worry lodged in her throat. "I think it's time to set up camp."

The fire burned blue.

Xanthe said the color came from the moss they used for kindling. It was perfectly normal—she'd been surprised to see *their* torches burn gold and white—but the bluish tint made the cave seem even more unnatural, painting the cavern in tones that belonged to an underwater world, a place of ocean, not earth.

Meilin stood watch at one side of the cave, her quarter-staff in her hands. Conor and Jhi rested nearby, while Takoda and Xanthe sat by the opposite wall.

Ahead of her, the path was darkness—no, people spoke of darkness, but this was something thicker—and it played tricks on her eyes, pulling her imagination toward unseen threats until she finally dragged her attention back to the cavern.

Takoda and Xanthe had their heads together near the fire, making shadow puppets on the cavern wall.

First, Takoda made a butterfly.

Then, Xanthe made a blob that was apparently some-thing called a snarle.

Next, Takoda made a bear.

Then, Xanthe made another blob with antennae she claimed was a gallor.

Takoda shook his head with a shy smile. "That's not a real thing."

Xanthe cocked her head, her pale hair glinting blue in the moss fire's light. "Just because you don't know what a snarle or a gallor is," she countered, "doesn't mean they aren't real." But there was a ghost of a smile at the edge of her mouth.

"You *are* making them up!"

Xanthe shrugged, but the smile widened. "Hey, you'd never seen a cyrix before either."

At that, Takoda shuddered dramatically. "And I hope I never see one again."

Kovo was supposed to be on watch, too, guarding the way they'd come, but the ape kept casting glances back at the pair by the fire.

He's jealous, thought Meilin. She was jealous, too, jealous of the way they could laugh, even now. She knew that if Rollan were here, he'd make her laugh. Or at least smile.

Conor whispered in his sleep. He lay curled against the cave wall nearby. Briggan had finally stopped pacing, and now stood sentry beside the boy while Jhi worked her silent, soothing power.

The strain had gone out of Conor's face, and his breathing had grown steady and even. He wasn't the only one calmed by the panda's presence. Meilin could feel her heart slowing, her panic ebbing as she lowered herself to the cool cave floor. She put her back to the wall, crossed her legs, and tried to breathe.

"I'll take watch," said Xanthe from the fire, casting a nervous glance at Conor as she spoke.

Anger still flared through Meilin, at Xanthe's fear, and the fact that she understood it.

She wanted to lash out, to hunt down Zerif and attack him for hurting her friend and endangering so many. Instead she was stuck here beneath the earth, watching Conor suffer. Feeling helpless. Useless. The anger and panic and fear were like ropes, wrapping themselves around her. She wanted to fight back, to tear free, but knew that struggling would only make the dark feelings tighten. Instead, she nodded, and tried to breathe, ground herself the way her fighting instructors had taught her, and let the ropes fall away.

Overhead, the blue light danced, and Jhi's calm wrapped around her. Eventually she felt her eyes begin to unfocus.

But as soon as they drifted shut, she heard a voice.

Not a stranger's voice, or an animal's, not the gurgle and rasp of the Many or the sound of water on the cave walls. It was a voice she knew too well. Her father's.

Meilin's eyes snapped open.

"Meilin," he called. The name echoed softly *". . . eilin . . . lin."*

It wasn't coming from the cavern, but from the tunnel beyond, a snaking path where the blue firelight quickly gave way to impenetrable black.

Meilin frowned, wondering if she'd imagined the sound, but then it came again.

"Meilin . . . eilin . . . lin. "

"Did you hear that?" she asked, turning back toward the fire, but there was no one there. No Takoda and Xanthe making shapes. No Kovo looming. No Conor and Briggan curled against the wall.

Only Jhi, sitting before the fire, her dark round shape like a shadow puppet, and her face blank in a way that reminded Meilin of that horrible sensation when their spirit animal bond had been stretched.

"Jhi?" she called. But the panda didn't look at her. Didn't blink.

"Meilin . . . eilin . . . lin," called her father. She knew it wasn't him, knew it couldn't be him, but there was so much strangeness here beneath the earth, and maybe, maybe, maybe . . .

Meilin got to her feet. She could feel Jhi's presence at her back, tugging, trying to keep her from following the sound, but Meilin had to know.

She called into the darkness. "Hello?"

Hello? Hello? Hello? It echoed.

But no other answer came.

Meilin took a step, out of the cave and into the tunnel, and then another, the blue light from the fire fading behind her until she could barely see the way ahead. Above her, roots pulsed like veins to a heart. As the tunnel sloped down beneath her feet, she knew it led toward the Evertree.

Every time she thought of stopping, the voice came again.

"Meilin . . . eilin . . . lin."

But now it didn't sound like her father.

It sounded like Zerif.

It sounded like Shane.

It sounded like Olvan.

It sounded like Conor.

It sounded like Abeke.

It sounded like Rollan.

It sounded like people she knew, and people she'd lost, and even people she hadn't met.

The ground beneath her feet became tangled with roots. The walls pressed in with them, and the tunnel became narrower and narrower, closing in until Meilin had to crawl on hands and knees toward the darkness at the heart of the world.

And then, all of a sudden, the tunnel gave way, and she was in a massive cavern, as big as the greatest hall in the largest fortress in Zhong.

She was kneeling on a stone floor, palms splayed, and under her fingers something had been gouged into the rock. Up close, it looked like a curve, but when she got to her feet, she gasped.

It was, of course, a spiral.

Meilin looked up, taking in the rest of the cavern.

The roots of the Evertree were *everywhere*. They wound around the edges of the space and over the floor. They climbed the walls and gathered together in the ceiling. Light streamed from every root, illuminating the strange chamber. A dozen of the strongest tendrils came together into a canopy overhead and trailed down like curtains in the middle of the cavern. *No*, Meilin realized, *not like curtains. Like* bars.

And standing there, in the center of the cage of roots, was a shape.

At first it seemed like a monster.

And then like a man.

And then like something else entirely.

Meilin knew just by looking at this *thing* that it was old, as old as the world, and as dark as the sky on a moonless night. Its presence seemed to soak up all the light and warmth, and radiate back a sickly cold.

It had no edges, and when it twisted toward her, she saw that it had no face.

And when it spoke, its voice whispered in her head, and the words all bled together like the rustle and crack and tread of the woods at night.

Meilin couldn't understand what it was saying, but it seemed *so very important*. Maybe, if she just got closer . . . She took a step, and the words got clearer. But she still couldn't understand, so she took another, and another, until she was right in front of the cage of roots.

The darkness smiled, and lunged.

Its hands shot forward through the bars and wrapped around her throat and—

Meilin sat forward with a gasp.

She was still sitting on the cavern floor at the mouth of the tunnel. Someone had cast a cloak over her like a blanket. Xanthe was crouching over her, her pink eyes bright, her small, pale hand resting on Meilin's arm.

"You were talking in your sleep," said Xanthe apologetically. Jhi sat a few feet away, gaze even but eyes dark. Had she seen it, too? The Wyrm? Meilin saw concern and sadness tinge the panda's steady eyes, as if she knew what waited for them in the dark.

I'm sorry, the panda seemed to say.

They were so different, Meilin and Jhi, like fire and earth. Meilin would never have guessed that their bond would stay strong even now, under such strain. Maybe it was *because* of their differences. Meilin and Jhi were still distinct, and often at odds, unlike Conor and Briggan, who seemed to share the same soul.

Meilin couldn't help but wonder how Rollan was faring.

The blue fire had gone cold, and Kovo was holding up their own revived golden torchlight while Takoda rolled a blanket back into his pack.

"We should get moving soon," said Xanthe. "It's still a ways to go. Oh, and I found some rockweed for us to eat," she added, holding out a ropy plant the color of seaweed.

Meilin could imagine Rollan saying, "Mmmm, delicious," in his sarcastic way. A pang went through her as she realized how much she missed him. She hoped he and Abeke were faring better on their own mission.

"Thanks," said Meilin, accepting the plant with dignity. She raised it to her mouth and hesitated.

"Best not to try and actually *eat* it," explained Xanthe. "The nutrients are in the juice. You chew on it, like this." Xanthe demonstrated, chewing on the stalk the way Meilin had seen farmers in the countryside do, trying to keep their mouths from going dry on the hottest days of harvest. It wasn't a very elegant process, but Meilin was crouching on a damp cave floor, her clothes stained with soil. There was a time for elegance, and a time for survival.

Besides, the rockweed actually tasted *good*, like honey and river water, and soon Meilin didn't care what she looked like, chewing the strange—fruit? vegetable?—food.

Across the cavern, Jhi and Kovo seemed to be engaged in a staring contest. The ape was much larger than the panda, but even he obviously wasn't immune to her influences, and Kovo was the first to break away, his red eyes escaping to the floor with a snort. Jhi made a small sound and rocked slightly, and if Meilin didn't know better, she'd think the panda was being smug.

"We need to get going," whispered Xanthe, tossing aside a spent stalk of rockweed.

Meilin didn't understand why the girl was keeping her voice low until she saw that Conor was still curled in the corner. Briggan's long body was stretched out beside him, like a barrier between the boy and the rest of the cave.

She hated to wake him, but the fact was that only reaching—and defeating—the Wyrm could save him. Jhi could slow the sickness, but the panda couldn't stop it.

Meilin got to her feet. Her whole body felt stiff, as if . . . well, as if she'd spent the night sitting on a cold cave floor. She flexed her muscles, aware of how long she'd gone without a proper fight—sure, there were plenty of things to run *from*—and how badly she wanted to avoid one.

She reached a hand toward Jhi. The panda considered her a moment before slowly bowing her head and vanishing in a burst of light and heat.

Meilin crossed the cave to Conor, but before she could reach out a hand, his eyes were drifting open.

Briggan stretched and nuzzled the boy's cheek.

"Hey there," he whispered, a tired smile tugging at his mouth.

"You're awake," said Meilin, kneeling beside him. "How are you feeling?"

Conor sat up and rubbed his head, the blond tufts standing up in a dozen directions. Before she could stop herself, Meilin reached out and smoothed the hair, feeling his forehead as casually as possible.

With Jhi's help, and a few hours of sleep, at least his fever was down again.

"What happened last night?" he asked.

"You got . . . sick," she said, searching for the right word.

His gaze went to his infected arm, folded against his ribs, and then to Xanthe, who was standing across the cavern, watching. "I'm sorry," he said. "I thought I could—"

"Conor, you should have said something."

He swallowed. "I'm already slowing us down."

"You have to tell us when it gets bad, okay? You have to tell *me*. That's what friends do."

He shook his head and wouldn't meet her eyes. When he spoke, his voice was sad and lost. "There's nothing you can do."

Meilin tensed.

There's nothing you can do.

They were her five least favorite words.

When Zhong had fallen, she'd heard them.

When her father had died, she'd heard them.

But she wouldn't accept those words, not now. Maybe she couldn't save Conor—not on her own, not without help and time and luck—but there *was* something she could do. She could stand at his side. She could be strong enough for both of them.

"You need to eat." Meilin handed him a stalk of rock-weed. "It's actually not bad," she said in response to his cautious look.

Briggan sniffed the plant, recoiled, and looked pitifully at Conor until he dug a scrap of dried meat from his sack.

"I can feel it," he whispered, turning the rockweed over in his hands.

She expected him to say the parasite, but instead he said, "The Wyrm. I can feel it here," he said, touching his arm. "But also there," he added, pointing down the tunnel

Meilin had guarded, the one she'd wandered in her sleep. "We're getting closer."

Every inch of Meilin's skin crawled at the thought of facing the monster from her dreams, but she forced herself to smile. "Good," she said, holding out her hand.

Conor took her hand and got to his feet, but he looked uncertain. "Is it?"

"Yes," said Meilin. "Because the sooner we get there, the sooner we can fight." She wrapped an arm around the boy's shoulders. "And the sooner we fight, the sooner we can *win*."

TROUBLE AT SEA

THE *TELLUN'S PRIDE II* CUT LIKE A KNIFE THROUGH THE waves, buoyed along by a strong current, a good wind, and a stretch of clear sky. It was a grand ship, and with the help of the breeze and the two whales at the bow pulling it along, they were well on their way to Stetriol.

"About time something went our way," said Rollan, turning his face toward the morning sun. "This weather is amazing!"

"Don't say that," warned Abeke. She was sitting cross-legged on a wooden crate, rolling an apple between her palms. "You'll jinx us."

"Come on," said Rollan, waving his hand. "How can I jinx us? There's not a cloud in the sky."

"I'm serious," she said. "Don't talk like that."

But now he couldn't help but tease her. "You know what?" he said. "I bet we get all the way to Stetriol without a drop of–" He was interrupted by the apple that Abeke lobbed at his head. Rollan dodged, and it caught him in the shoulder instead. There wasn't much force behind the blow, and he finished defiantly, "*–rain.*"

Abeke shook her head as he rubbed his shoulder where the apple had struck.

"*Tenavo*," she said.

"What's that?" he asked.

"That was the word for bad luck in my village. Not just any bad luck, but the kind you ask for."

"Superstitious girl," grumbled Rollan, fetching up the fallen apple. He took a big bite.

"You'll see," she warned.

Ten minutes later, the storm rolled in.

They stood at the rail, watching it form on the horizon. It approached at first like a malevolent ship, and then something much bigger than a ship, and then a *wall*.

Within minutes, the storm was on them, and it was raging. It swallowed up the blue sky, carrying clouds that went from white, to gray, to charcoal. Thunder rumbled through them, and lightning danced, and then the rain came, crashing down like a wave.

Within seconds, they were soaked through.

Rollan craned his head back, squinting through the icy rain. "Essix!" he called up into the worsening storm, but the bird was nowhere to be seen. She probably had the good sense to get above the clouds. Right about now, as the ship rocked under the growing swells and shuddered under the force of the rain, Rollan was wishing he could do the same.

He had seen his fair share of bad weather, but he'd always been on land, crouched under an awning or in a doorway, tucked behind some bins or under a set of stairs. He'd never been in the middle of it.

Now, standing on the deck of the *Tellun's Pride II*, he didn't have much choice.

The downpour battered the deck and crashed against the hull, the ship bucking like an angry horse beneath them. Soon it was all they could do to stay on their feet.

Abeke glared at Rollan. *"Tenavo!"* she repeated, the word sounding more like a curse as she shouted at him through the gusts of wind and torrents of rain.

The crew, most of them caught just as off guard by the sudden storm, now scrambled over the deck, tying down all the cargo, tarping the crates, and collapsing the sails. Abeke and Rollan helped to drop an anchor so they wouldn't be hurled off course, but the rope got stuck in its crank, and as they heaved at it, they both nearly went overboard.

"Get inside," ordered a stocky Greencloak as Rollan slipped and slid on the waterlogged deck and Abeke fought to keep her own balance. "Before you're washed away."

They sat in silence at a table in the ship's galley. Their clothes were soaked through, dripping water on the table, the bench, the floor. A few other Greencloaks sat at the table, too, most of them looking just as bedraggled.

Abeke stared across at Rollan. Her dark skin had a greenish tint from the sloshing of the waves. She was nursing a glass of juice instead of food, and obviously waiting for him to say something. Her fingers tapped out a beat on the table, and even though the sound was lost beneath the groan of the ship, he could feel her tension. She was as coiled as a cat.

"Well?" she said at last.

Rollan fidgeted damply. He looked up at the ceiling, at a lamp swaying on its hook. A drop of icy rain dripped from his hair and slid beneath his collar. He shivered, wondering if he would ever be dry again. More rainwater dripped from his hair into his soup. "Well?" he echoed.

"Are you going to apologize?"

"For what?"

Abeke let out an exasperated sound. Rollan had to fight back a smile—it was the kind of noise Meilin would make. "I told you," said Abeke sharply. "I told you not to test our luck. Am I such a superstitious girl now?"

"Fine, fine," said Rollan, rolling his eyes. *"Tenavo."*

Abeke blew out her breath and said something in her native tongue. Even though Rollan didn't know the words, he got the idea. She brought her head to rest on her arms, Uraza's tattoo crouched across her skin.

He chewed his cheek. "Okay, so how do you undo it?" he asked, running a hand through his wet hair. "This *tenavo*?"

Abeke glanced up, the ghost of humor in her eyes.

"I mean," he went on, "assuming it exists, and assuming *someone* is noble and selfless enough to try and undo its effects even though he definitely didn't cause it, what would they have to do?"

"Well," she said thoughtfully. "They would have to do the magical *intenavo* dance."

Rollan's eyes narrowed with skepticism. "Is that so?"

"Indeed," said Abeke, nodding gravely.

"And how would someone do this *intenavo* dance?"

Abeke looked around. She got to her feet and plucked some dried herbs from the wall, bracing herself against the counter when a particularly bad swell made the ship sway.

"We normally use flowers, but these will have to do." She plucked a few colorful herbs and stuck them in Rollan's wet hair. "Now you get up, and hold out your arms and bounce up and down on your toes five times, then move your hips in a circle, all while saying, 'Forgive me, Great Tenavo. I am a foolish boy.'"

Rollan looked at her skeptically. "And that will help?"

Abeke shrugged. "It couldn't hurt."

The Greencloaks at the other end of the table were watching with amusement. Rollan felt his face go red. But he took a deep breath, and he did it. He got to his feet, and held his arms toward the ceiling, and bounced on his toes, and swiveled his hips, and said the words.

After the first round, the sky bellowed with thunder, and Abeke said he should probably try again.

"I don't think it's working," sighed Rollan, sagging back onto the bench after the third or fourth attempt.

Abeke was sitting on the bench, smothering a fit of giggles behind her hand. Rollan could feel a smile working its way onto his own face. He didn't mind being silly, if it made Abeke smile. Ever since they'd faced Zerif in the forest, she'd been closed off, distracted. "You did your best," she said, stifling a laugh.

The galley door flew open, and the captain and first mate blew in.

"I see you two got caught in it, too." Arac's voice carried ahead of him through the room.

"Quite a storm out there," said Nisha, a few steps behind. They both had had the good sense to trade their greens for hooded weatherproof cloaks. A handful of Greencloaks trailed in behind them, a stream of seawater in their wake.

"Came out of nowhere, didn't it?" chimed in Arac. "Someone must have challenged the sea."

Abeke shot Rollan a look, and Rollan ducked his head over his food.

"Arrogant thing, the sea," continued Arac, fixing himself a bowl. "Can't help but rise to a challenge."

Rollan gripped his bowl.

"Gotta be careful what you say around it."

"It was my fault, okay?!" announced Rollan. "I did it!"

The other Greencloaks shot him a variety of looks, some amused, others annoyed, all damp.

Arac only chuckled. "Should've known."

"If a ship can't weather a storm," said Nisha, "it isn't much of a ship." She offered Rollan a wink, and he felt his shoulders relax. The captain scrunched up her nose. "Are those bay leaves in your hair?"

Rollan was about to explain about the luck-restoring ritual when he felt something move around his feet, and then a dark shape leaped up onto the bench, vanished again, and appeared on the table in front of him, holding what was left of his chunk of bread.

It was a spider monkey.

Arac's spider monkey, judging by its mischievous expression and the fact the man's tattoo was now missing from his chest. Before Rollan could reach for his bread, the monkey was off again, scaling Arac's arm to perch on his shoulder.

"Nexi," said Arac, by way of introduction. The spider monkey tipped its head.

Rollan glanced at Nisha, who was pouring herself some soup.

"Where's your parrot?" he asked before he could stop himself. Nisha gave him a knowing look.

"It's a little cliché, don't you think? A captain strolling around a ship with a parrot on her shoulder?"

"All you need is an eye patch," offered Rollan cheerfully. "Or a wooden leg."

Nisha chuckled good-naturedly. "Truth be told, Relis doesn't care much for the open water. Besides . . ." Her expression darkened. "I'm sure you've felt the strain. I feel better keeping him close, until we find a way to fix it."

"That's probably a good idea . . ." Rollan looked up at the ceiling and wondered where Essix was. He'd been scared to test their connection. Scared Essix would pull away. As long as he let her roam free, he could pretend everything was still okay between them. He didn't have to find out if it wasn't.

"What about you, Arac?" asked Abeke. "You don't feel the same?"

Arac snorted. "I'd like to see you try and make Nexi do anything she doesn't want to do." The spider monkey, who'd been busy hiding bits of bread in Arac's blond ponytail, looked up at the mention of her name, flashed a grin full of teeth, then went back to work.

Nisha came over, carrying two bowls of soup and spilling neither—which Rollan thought was seriously impressive, considering how much the ship was swaying.

"It'll calm," she said, casting a look at Abeke, who was clutching the table's edge. "These kinds of storms, they don't last long."

The captain sat, pushing the second bowl of soup in her husband's direction. "Before you know it, we'll be in Stetriol."

Rollan's gaze went to their sodden green cloaks, hanging on hooks along the galley wall.

"Still not sure how good I feel about wearing green over there," he said. "Feels a bit too much like wearing a target on my back."

"Olvan said—" started Abeke.

"I know, I know," said Rollan. "It's just . . . does Olvan even *know* what Stetriol's really like these days? Has he been there himself?"

"*We* have," said Nisha, nodding at Arac.

"Really?" asked Abeke. "What's it like?"

"Weird," grunted Arac.

"Different," said Nisha at the same time. "Better." Arac grumbled something unintelligible into his bowl as he drank down the rest of the soup.

"What was that?" challenged Nisha.

Arac set down the empty wooden bowl with a thud. "I said it's still *Stetriol*."

Nisha shook her head, as if they'd had this conversation before. "Arac."

"I lost my brother to the Conquerors," said the man.

"We all lost someone," countered Nisha. "That is the nature of war. But if we keep looking back, we'll never move forward." She turned her attention to Rollan and Abeke. "It's amazing, the difference. You won't even recognize it. It's not just about what's there, it's about what's *not*. The air is different, clearer. The people are healthier and happier. It still has a ways to go, but it *is* progress."

Rollan pushed his bowl aside. "Maybe they should rename it. To help people forget."

The captain shook her head. "They don't want to erase the past, Rollan. They just want to move on. And we can help them. So much is changing in Erdas, and most of it for the worse, but Stetriol is changing for the better. And that's something."

Silence fell over the galley.

"Do you feel that?" asked Nisha, cocking her head.

Rollan didn't. "No."

"Exactly," she said with a smile. He realized then that he didn't feel the ship swaying, didn't hear the wind and rain barreling the sides and sails.

"The storm," he said. "It's over."

THE DANGEROUS DEEP

THE STORM HAD INDEED PASSED.

Not slowly, but all at once, just as it had come.

Standing on deck, Abeke could see the dark mass of clouds moving away, retreating like a curtain of shadow across the sea, leaving still, blue sky in its wake. "Fickle thing, the sea," said Arac. "Isn't it?"

Abeke smiled and shot a look at Rollan beside her, but he only shook his head, dislodging the last few bay leaves she'd stuck in his hair. They fluttered down to the deck. "No way," he said. "I'm officially done goading the ocean. From here on out, I plan to tell it how nice it looks, and how much I respect its prowess."

Abeke laughed and looked around. The change *was* kind of incredible. With the bad weather gone, the sea glittered in the light. It reminded her of the Niloan grasslands after the sun came up and before the dew burned off, when everything was still wet. It didn't seem possible—after all, they were on the ocean, *everything* was wet—but that was how she thought of it. Sparkling. Fresh. Even the air tasted better, less like salt and more like, well, *air.*

Abeke drew in a deep breath just as a screech sounded overhead. Relief flooded Rollan's face, and moments later, Essix dove, landing on the boy's shoulder, her talons digging into the wool of his cloak.

"Maybe we should get *you* an eye patch," teased Nisha.

"Only if you make me captain," countered Rollan with a grin. He touched his temple against the bird's crown, and Essix took wing again, sweeping over Arac's head. The gyrfalcon plucked a piece of soggy bread from the man's ponytail before banking up again.

"And I thought Nexi had a mind of her own," Arac mumbled as the bird landed on the mast. His attention turned to Abeke. "When are we going to see that Uraza of yours?" he asked.

Abeke's chest tightened, her hand brushing the tattoo on her arm. "I imagine when we're back on—"

But she was cut off by a terrible sound, like a drowning cry, and the horrible give beneath her feet as the ship torqued sharply to one side.

"Did we hit something?" asked Rollan. But the ship hadn't stopped. It was still pressing forward in a halting way, jerking side to side as it did.

Even the most experienced sailors stumbled, fighting for balance, and calls of alarm went up across the deck. Abeke dropped instinctively into a crouch, but before she could catch Rollan's sleeve, he went down hard on his hands and knees as the ship groaned beneath them. Luckily most of the cargo was still tied down from the storms, but the people weren't.

"What's going on?" shouted Nisha, who was somehow upright and moving swiftly across the deck.

Just then the ship rocked heavily, as if hit sideways by a massive wave. Even in the midst of the storm it hadn't swayed this much. Now, as it careened between the bright sun and calm sea, Abeke knew that something must be very wrong.

"The whales!" demanded the captain. "See to the whales!"

Abeke stayed crouched, clutching the base of a nearby rope for support, but Rollan struggled to his feet.

"Stay low!" she called, sensing another shudder from the ship. But he didn't hear her; he was already up. He made it halfway to the bow before the spasm came. The ship hurled forward and Rollan went down like before, but this time the deck wasn't flat beneath him. The whole thing was banking steeply to the right, ocean spraying up in a cold mist.

And when Rollan fell, he slid.

The deck was still slick from rain, and he skidded toward the rail. Abeke let go of her rope and lunged for him, skinning her knees and catching his wrist before he could slide beneath the wooden rail and crash down into the deep.

"I've got you," she said, panic flooding her as she felt her grip begin to slip. But the ship was already tilting back the other way, and they managed to scramble away from the edge.

Rollan was gasping for air, but his eyes were still fixed on the rail. "Did you see that?"

"See what?" she asked, breathless.

"There was something down there. In the water. I thought I saw a—"

But his words were lost as the ship shuddered again, and Nisha's orders broke their attention.

They got to their feet; by the time they reached the bow, they found half the crew struggling with the lines that held the whales in place. One of the two beasts was pulling the craft sideways as it tried to escape the second, which was thrashing and writhing against some invisible attacker beneath the current. Abeke scanned the water in search of sharks, or eels, some trace of blood, but there were no signs of whatever was attacking the whale. It dove, or tried to, but the harness binding it to the *Tellun's Pride II* held, and the ship bobbed dangerously, like an apple dropped into a bucket.

There was a cry, and two men nearly went over, clinging to ropes and rails for support as others rushed to haul them back on board. The whale kept twisting and turning, as if possessed. It was obviously losing strength—but it might still have enough to wreck the ship before it tired.

"What's wrong with it?" asked Rollan.

"It must be hurt!" said Abeke.

"Cut it loose!" ordered Nisha, but no one seemed able to get close enough. The harness had gotten tangled during the whale's panic. "Cut it loose before it sinks the whole ship!"

Arac was at the bow, calling out orders, sawing at the ropes as fast as he could. But the storm had left them wet, the knots swollen with rainwater. He dulled one blade on the waterlogged ropes, cast it aside, demanded another.

"It's not giving, Nisha! We'll have to unfasten the harnesses from the whale's end."

Abeke was already swinging a leg over the side, getting ready to jump into the roiling sea.

"Wait!" cried Rollan, and she could see he was still shaken from whatever he'd seen in the water. Abeke hesitated.

But Nisha didn't.

The captain tore off her cloak and swung her legs over the railing, a knife already out and clutched in her grip. She dove with the experienced grace of a lifelong swimmer over the ship's side and into the water below. Arac paled when his wife went over but didn't abandon his work.

Rollan drew his own short knife and set to sawing beside Arac, casting glances every few seconds at the churning waters where the whale still thrashed. One of the ropes of the harness finally broke, but the metal hook on the other had warped, pinning it to the ship. Beneath the current, Abeke could see Nisha's shape moving alongside the panicked whale. She hadn't even come up for air.

"Swims like a fish, my wife," said Arac, his voice tight with pride and fear.

All of a sudden, the rope went slack. Far below, Nisha must have finally gotten the harness from the raging creature. The ship stopped bucking and rocked to a halt, the world evening out around Abeke. She hadn't realized how much it was churning until it went still. The wounded whale didn't surface. Instead it dove, a dark shape disappearing into the depths of the sea, and an instant later, Nisha broke the surface of the water, gasping for air.

Abeke felt *herself* gasp with relief, and then realized every other hand on board was sighing, too.

A pair of Greencloaks was throwing a rope ladder over the side, and Nisha scaled it, taking half the ocean with her. Water ran down her limbs and over her clothes as she ascended, her face drawn. When she hoisted herself back over the ship's rail, water pooled at her feet and a woman rushed forward with a coarse towel.

"A bit brisk for a swim," said the captain, teeth chattering, and everyone laughed, but the air was still tense with confusion.

"What happened?" asked Arac, his voice and gaze searching.

"Was it ill?" asked another.

"Was it injured?"

"Was it mad?"

"Was it frightened?"

"What could have possessed it so?"

The questions came in a wave, and Nisha held up her hand for order. "Be calm." But something was wrong, thought Abeke. She could see it in the captain's eyes, in the way she leaned back against the rail, not just for breath, but for strength. She didn't know what had happened beneath the current, but she could see that the captain was shaken. Badly.

She shot a look at Rollan and saw his face tight with concern. Whatever was wrong with the captain, he'd seen it, too.

"The whale wasn't simply frightened," explained Nisha. "Something attacked it."

Rollan went pale, and Abeke wondered what he'd seen moving beneath the surface.

"A shark?"

"A sea eel?"

"But there was no blood in the water," pressed Arac.

Nisha was shaking her head. "Because the whale wasn't bleeding."

"I thought you said it was being attacked."

"It was." When Nisha spoke, the words seemed to take a lot of effort. "There were no teeth marks. No claws. No wounds."

"Then how—"

"It was being attacked from the *inside*."

"How do you know?" asked an older Greencloak.

"Because I *saw* the thing attacking it," said Nisha grimly. "I saw it moving beneath the whale's skin."

Abeke went very cold.

"I tried to cut it out," Nisha continued. "But it was no use. When my knife cut through, it . . . it became two."

At that, Nisha gritted her teeth and held out her hand. It had been curled into a fist at her side while she spoke, but as her fingers peeled away to reveal her palm, Abeke saw something that made her heart turn.

She heard Rollan's breath catch in horror beside her.

In the center of Nisha's palm was a small dark mark.

A spiral was buried in her skin.

A *parasite*. Behind Abeke's eyes, she saw Conor's outstretched arm, the horrible mark that seemed to twitch beneath his skin, stealing time and life and sanity. No. No. Not this. Not again.

Arac must have recognized it, too, because the man let out a strangled sound of fury as the parasite writhed and wound its way up Nisha's palm and over her wrist.

"I tried to . . ." The captain trailed off, swaying on her feet even though the deck was now steady. Arac was there to catch her before she could fall.

"Nisha, Nisha, stay with me," demanded Arac as the captain shivered against him. "Where's Gera?" he shouted, calling for the Greencloak's medic.

The woman was already pushing her way through the gathered crowd, kneeling in front of them and tearing strips of cloth to bind around Nisha's elbow, as if the parasite could be contained by a simple tourniquet.

"Get back," Arac growled as the crew pressed in. Abeke didn't realize she'd been edging forward, too, until she felt Rollan's hand on her arm. The weight of his touch was a comfort, a sign of solidarity as much as a barricade, holding her at bay.

She watched as Gera drew a knife and pressed the tip into the captain's forearm, skewering the dark shape that writhed beneath the surface.

"I've got it, I've got it," said Gera. And that's when Abeke realized that Gera didn't know how sinister the parasites were, how infectious. The medic let out a sound of dismay as, to everyone's horror—everyone's horror and Abeke's sadness—the parasite divided in two once more, half still burrowing up Nisha's arm, the other half now snaking quickly up the medic's blade, right for her fingers. Gera cast the knife aside before the creature could reach her hand, and Rollan kicked it over the ship's edge and into the sea.

Abeke felt ill—how many other creatures would become infected by that squirming shadow? How quickly would the evil spread?

Blood streamed from the wound in Nisha's arm. The dark shape beneath her skin continued upward, slower, but otherwise undeterred.

"Gera," growled Arac. "There has to be something . . ."

"It's no use," said the medic, shaking her head. "I'm sorry."

"It's okay," breathed Nisha. "I'm okay. I'm okay. I'm okay."

But the words sounded hollow, the repetitions of someone slipping into a fever. How long would she last? And if–*when*, realized Abeke with horror–she fell victim, could she ever find her way back? If–*when*–they defeated Zerif and stopped the mysterious Wyrm, what would happen to those who'd already fallen? Was there hope?

Arac swept the captain into his arms and set off toward the steps down into the ship's hold, leaving behind only a trail of seawater from Nisha's clothes. Abeke looked down at the nearest puddle and saw a drop of blood swirling in the middle of the salty stain. She watched the red twist and spread, feeling helpless and scared and desperate to reach Stetriol, to do something instead of watch those she cared about suffer. Her body tensed. Her stomach turned.

And then Abeke felt Rollan take her hand. The two stood there, as motionless as the rest of the crew on the rocking deck.

"We have to stop this," she whispered.

"We will," said Rollan, his voice laced with fear, but also grim determination.

The Greencloaks stood vigil on the deck for several long minutes before Arac reemerged, looking pale. A streak of his wife's blood stained his sleeve.

"She's resting," he announced distantly. He was standing there among them, but Abeke could tell that his thoughts were still belowdecks, with Nisha. "She's strong," he added, lower. "She's a fighter." He blinked a few times—focused, glared, straightened. "What are you all standing around for? Get this ship back on course!"

"Sir," said a short, balding Greencloak as Arac turned away. "What should we do about the second whale?"

Arac looked back and shook his head.

"Cut it loose," he grumbled. "It can't pull the ship alone. They work in pairs. One's no good without the other."

THE LEFT PATH

THEY KEPT CONOR IN THE MIDDLE.

It was the only way to keep him from falling behind, and the only way to keep Meilin herself from falling over, since when he was at the back of the pack she kept looking over her shoulder to check on him, until she inevitably stumbled on a root or a rock. She had the scuffed palms and bruised knees to show for it.

But it was more than that.

With Conor holding the torchlight in front of her—Xanthe didn't want it in her eyes, said it was too "red bright," whatever that meant—Meilin could watch his movements. She kept track of when his legs began to drag, when his body began to sway. The fact was, if *he* wouldn't tell them when he was tired, she'd have to do it herself. Meilin knew he was afraid of slowing them down. He murmured as much when he was curled up between Jhi and Briggan, sick with fever and fatigue. But she wasn't going to speed up, not if it meant losing him.

Meilin would keep Conor with them, keep him *Conor*, for as long as she could.

For as long as she had to.

Behind her, Takoda and Kovo signed messages to one another in eerie silence. Meilin didn't like having the ape where she couldn't watch him, but this stretch of tunnel was narrow, and if he went ahead, his wall of black fur blocked out the light. Meanwhile, up at the front of the group, Xanthe was humming.

It was a strange tune that got picked up not only by the rock walls, but by the moss and mushrooms and the shallow pools as well, carrying through the tunnels like a gust of air. Now and then there were words in the song, words in a language Meilin didn't know. It made her think of the creature that whispered in her dreams. She wondered if the words were muffled, as they'd seemed, or if they were another language. One as old as the rustling of leaves and the rushing of water in a stream. One as old as the world itself.

Just then, as her thoughts were lost in deciphering dreams, something reached out and brushed Meilin's arm. She caught her breath and spun, slashing with her quarterstaff and pinning the attacker back, before she realized that it wasn't an attacker at all, only a tendril of root that had come loose from the tunnel ceiling.

Meilin let out a shuddering breath.

"You show that tree," said Takoda with a mock frown.

Meilin scowled back, then realized he was mimicking her. Kovo snorted. Xanthe chuckled, and even Conor managed a weak smile. Meilin blew her hair out of her eyes. Too long underground. It was making her paranoid. She lowered her quarterstaff and stepped up closer to examine the offending root.

The ropy strand was thicker than any of the ones she'd seen so far. Once, they'd been little more than thin cords that ran like cracks in the ceiling overhead. Now some roots were as thick as her wrist, others as big as her upper arm. And up close, she could see that the root—all the roots—were *moving*. Not quickly, but not as slowly as stars either. They moved like a body shifting in sleep, loosing fragments of earth and rock with every small twist and turn.

The sound of crumbling stones was eerie, like skittering feet, and Meilin found herself wishing that Xanthe would start humming again—anything to distract from the feeling that they were not only underneath the earth, but inside a living thing. A dying thing.

Meilin shuddered and turned back to find that the group had stopped. At first she thought they were waiting for her. Then she realized, with a flicker of annoyance, they were waiting for *Xanthe*, who'd paused up ahead. Meilin frowned. The only thing she disliked more than not leading was not being *able* to lead. She hated that she didn't know this underground world, that all she could do was follow.

Up ahead of Xanthe, the tunnel branched suddenly into two identical paths. At least, they looked identical to Meilin. She watched as the girl closed her eyes and brought her pale fingertips to the stone divide between the tunnels. What could she tell, just by touching the wall? Meilin had seen her do this a dozen times, had even tried to mimic it, pressing her hand to the rocks now and then, but she never felt anything except the cold damp of the cave.

But Xanthe must have felt something, because a moment later, her hand fell away and her pink eyes drifted open. She didn't speak, though. Her pale face remained contorted with concentration as she tipped her head from side to side, trying to process what she'd learned.

"Well?" prompted Meilin.

"It's strange," said Xanthe. "But both paths lead where we are going, in the end . . ." She trailed off in a way that made Meilin think there was something she wasn't saying.

"So what's the difference?" asked Meilin, but Xanthe didn't answer. She was already plunging into the tunnel on the left, and the group had no choice but to follow her into the dark.

It was an easy road compared to the ones they'd taken so far, a gentle slope with weedy yellow mushrooms sprouting from the seam where the curved walls met the floor. Like many of the fungi here in Sadre, the tops glowed faintly with their own internal light, not enough to see by, just enough to stand out against the surrounding rock, the way clouds did sometimes when the moon was bright.

Xanthe led the way, not even bothering to look back. That prickle of annoyance began to rise in Meilin again at the thought of being helpless. She couldn't cure Conor. She couldn't find the Evertree's roots. But then she felt Jhi's touch, like a paw against the center of her back, and she remembered something her father had told her years before, when Meilin said she wanted to be like him, a warrior.

"What kind of warrior?" he'd asked.

"The kind that leads," she'd answered proudly.

"Then first you will learn to be a foot soldier."

Needless to say, Meilin had not been pleased. "But I want to be a *leader*," she'd insisted, as if he'd misunderstood her answer.

"That may be," he'd said, "but a true leader knows when to follow."

Meilin straightened and stared at Xanthe, who walked ahead like a pale, wavering flame in the dark. Solitary.

Alone, thought Meilin.

With Phos Astos gone, Xanthe was alone. No family. No spirit animal. And yet, the girl hadn't stopped to mourn, hadn't hesitated. Even after she found out about Conor, she was still here, still helping. Maybe she needed this mission as much as any of them. After all, her world was in danger, too.

What they had to do was more important than either one of them, and if they were going to succeed, they would need to work together. And if that meant Meilin needed to follow instead of lead, then all right.

Besides, thought Meilin with a grim smile, *Xanthe may be the one who gets us to the Wyrm in one piece, but once we're there, I'll be the one to defeat it.*

"Hey, there's light up ahead," called Takoda.

Meilin blinked, dragging herself out of the bright world of memory and back into the darkened tunnel.

Jhi's touch faded from her mind, replaced by a quickening pulse.

Takoda was right. Light was beginning to dance on the cave walls ahead, low and flickering. It was faint, so faint that the old Meilin wouldn't have noticed it. Even if her muscles were stiff from lack of training, the weeks beneath the earth were sharpening her sight.

"I can hear water," murmured Conor.

"Maybe there's a village," added Meilin, thinking how nice it would be to see new faces. To eat something that looked like food, and sleep on something that wasn't stone. She chided herself. She'd never been a soft girl, had always been able to hold her own with the soldiers, but what she wouldn't give right now for a bath, a bed.

"There's no village this way," said Xanthe, her voice tense. "The glow must be coming from stone moss and river fern . . ."

"Do you hear that?" asked Takoda from just behind Meilin.

"The water?" prompted Conor.

"No," said Takoda. "There's something else."

And when Meilin strained to hear over the slosh and burble, she heard it, too, though she didn't know what it was. The skittering of loose pebbles? The shuffle of steps?

Briggan's ears twitched, and his lips curled in warning, his wolfish blue eyes bright. Conor's torchlight snagged on something on the wall. Meilin reached out and brushed her fingers over the damp surface. The rock was softer here, and strangely grooved. She fit her fingertips to the lines and traced their course, and then recoiled as she realized how easily her nails had fit the grooves.

The ground was getting slicker, too. When she looked down, she noticed that it was a mess of crushed yellow mushrooms, trampled underfoot. Though Conor and Xanthe had been walking ahead of her, Meilin knew they hadn't done this damage, not alone. This was the work of dozens of feet, maybe more.

"You guys," she murmured. "Something isn't—"

Xanthe's breath caught audibly in her throat. She'd nearly reached the mouth of the tunnel when she froze. When the others caught up and saw what she saw, a sickly silence settled over them.

The mouth of the cave opened into the wall of a large cavern. Spikes of rock—stalagmites and stalactites—jutted up from ground and down from ceiling, transforming the cavern into a gaping mouth with flashing rows of sharpened teeth.

But it wasn't the illusion of a predator's fangs that stopped them cold.

It was what waited beyond them. Because there, behind the wall of spiking teeth, were the Many.

Tens.

Hundreds.

A writhing mass of bodies, pale and wormy and marked by black pulsing spirals. As thick as rats on a sewer floor.

Conor gasped and tossed the torchlight back into the tunnel behind them as if burned, plunging them into shadow an instant before one of the creatures looked up. Its milky eyes panned across the cavern walls. Meilin's heart pounded as its gaze brushed across them like a chill.

"Don't move," whispered Xanthe. The order passed back through the ranks like an echo.

Look away, thought Meilin to the creature. *Look away. Look away.*

But the creature was at the edge of the tangled horde, and *something* had caught its attention. It stared, fixated, up at them, its face blank, eyes unblinking. Meilin wished Xanthe weren't at the front of the pack, with her skin so pale it caught every flicker of light.

Meilin's fingers tightened on her quarterstaff.

It was a ten-foot drop from their perch at the mouth of the tunnel into the cavern's jaws below, and Meilin could see the marks in the mud where the bodies of the Many had slipped and slid. The slope was so steep it would be almost impossible for one to climb back up. But Meilin didn't think the Many cared about impossible. She could picture the creatures clambering toward them anyway, with their empty eyes and their mindless, tireless pursuit. Could picture them climbing over and on top of each other, turning bodies into stairs until they reached the tunnel.

Beside Meilin, Conor shuddered. It was a small, involuntary motion, but the creature below cocked its head and took a shuffling step forward. Its hand drifted up through the air, the gesture in slow motion, as if the limb were underwater. But as it opened its mouth, another pale form jostled it from behind.

Just like that, the spell was broken.

The creature spun on its assailant, and the two went down in a shuffling mess of limbs. No one tried to pull them apart. No one even noticed. Within moments, their bodies were swallowed up by the rest of the Many, who walked right over them as if they were rocks.

Up in the tunnel, Xanthe braved a single step backward, the others moving with her, inching away from the edge, and the flickering light, and the mass of pale limbs and teeth. Only once they'd all edged back to the discarded torch did they *run*.

Back past the trampled mushrooms and the claw marks on the wall, back through the winding tunnel, back to the chamber where the two paths split, and they'd chosen left.

They stood in a circle, breathless.

Meilin's fingers ached from clutching her staff.

All the color had drained from Conor's face, though she didn't know if it was from fatigue or the sight of the terrible creatures with the spirals in their skin.

Kovo glared back down the tunnel, his red eyes narrowed on the dark.

Takoda had a hand on Xanthe's shoulder. The girl's narrow arms were wrapped around herself.

"Okay, new plan," said Meilin, "we take the other path."

Takoda and Conor nodded, but, if it was possible, Xanthe's pale skin got even whiter. Her pink eyes widened.

"What's wrong?" pressed Meilin. "You said they both lead to where we're going."

"They do," said Xanthe slowly. "But *that* . . ." she said, pointing to the left route, the one they'd chosen, the one filled with the Many, ". . . was the *easy* path."

Meilin swallowed, and looked to the divide. The other path spiraled away into darkness.

They had no choice, but the question hung unspoken in the air, as heavy as smoke.

If the left path was supposed to be the easy one, then what could possibly be waiting for them on the right?

STETRIOL'S WELCOME

"**L**and!"

The call went up just before noon.

The *Tellun's Pride II* had been slowed by the loss of its whales but was spurred forward by a strong current and a merciful wind behind its sails.

Now Stetriol loomed, growing larger and closer by the minute. Abeke had never seen the capital before, didn't know what it had looked like during the time of the Bile and the Conquerors, but she'd heard stories, and she could tell from the energy that this was a new world. And hopefully a better one.

Abeke clutched a slip of paper. Word had arrived from Greenhaven that morning, written in Olvan's hand but bound to a messenger bird with Lenori's yellow ribbon. According to the healer at the Evertree, their friends were still alive somewhere beneath its roots. That was all she could say.

Stay strong, Olvan had instructed. *Focus on your mission.*

Arac stood at the ship's bow, calling out orders while Nisha leaned against the mast, ill but upright. Word was her husband had tried to keep her in her cabin, and she'd given him a verbal lashing. The sounds of the fight had rung out through the ship, most of the words lost, but the meaning known: Nisha would be captain until the moment the sickness took her. And staying cooped up in her cabin would do nothing to slow its course.

Her parrot, Relis, sat on her shoulder, its rainbow feathers flustered and its black eyes heavy, knowing. Would the parrot stay with the captain until the end? What then? Nisha's dark arms, lean but strong, were bare beneath her cloak. Abeke saw shallow cuts running up her right arm like notches in a tree. Gera, the medic, had obviously tried to stop the parasite's progress, tried to cut it from the captain's skin. In the end, she'd only bought Nisha a little time—Abeke saw the trace of the black spiral already against the base of the captain's throat. Nisha was holding on, but Abeke could tell she was losing the fight. Slowly, yes, but faster than Conor. Too much of the parasite had escaped the medic's blade. Sweat beaded on her brow, and her once radiant skin had taken on a sickly pallor.

How can something so small do so much damage? marveled Abeke sadly.

But of course, she knew. Not all enemies were large.

Back in Nilo, she had seen a man die of infection.

He'd been wounded on a hunt, not badly, barely a graze along his calf. The cut was so shallow that no one even thought to treat it. Besides, he was one of the strongest men in her village, strong as an ox, an elk, a tiger. He was a tree, a mountain, and he laughed off the small cut, called it a bug bite, a splinter, a nick.

But the night after he was injured, the man trod through a puddle of stagnant water, and by morning, the line was angry and red, the skin hot to the touch. Still he waved away the ministrations of their healers. By the third day, vicious red lines wove up his leg from the cut, now infected. And by the fourth, the sickness was in his blood.

Such a small wound—a nick—had felled a mountain of a man.

"You ready?" asked Rollan, appearing beside her. He'd followed her gaze and must have thought she was looking at the approaching city, not the captain before it.

Abeke nodded as the ship entered the port.

Stetriol's docks were alive with motion and noise. Up and down their length, sailors called out, men traded words and wares, and carts moved crates. Abeke saw two other ships with Greencloak flags, and mixed among them were ferries from Zhong and Eura, and even one from as far as Amaya. In the bay, a handful of whales and dolphins and rays swam in circles, and on the docks she saw horses, cats, and dogs, some with the focused gaze of spirit animals and others the more docile look of pets. Calls went up, and ropes were flung onto the docks, caught by workers who helped to haul the *Tellun's Pride II* into its berth.

Arac and Nisha were quarreling again in hushed tones. Abeke tried not to overhear, but Rollan was obviously making no such attempt, because he leaned over to whisper in her ear.

"Arac wants Nisha to go ashore for help. And Nisha refuses to leave the ship. So Arac says he'll stay with her, and she says he's to go ahead with us, and—"

At that point in the conversation, Arac stormed away, muttering curses and kicking a crate. Nisha glared after him, then sank back against the mast, looking exhausted.

Word of their arrival had landed ahead of them, and many people were gathering around the docks. Abeke could feel Rollan tense beside her, donning his own hostility like armor against an impending fight. But there was no malice in the people's faces that she could see. No distrust. Only curiosity, and here and there, even a smile of delight. And throughout the crowd, the first traces of spirit animals bonded without Bile. A girl held a blue-eyed cat close to her chest. A boy cupped a turtle in his hands.

Things change, Abeke reminded herself. *And we are part of that change.*

Half a dozen Greencloaks stood waiting on the docks, their crisp mantles shining emerald in the midday sun. Tattoos peeked over collars and out of cuffs, and a green-eyed lemur sat on one man's shoulder, a small dog beside another's boot. Beside the Greencloaks, a second set of men and women, these dressed in blue and black, stood at equal attention. Silver pins with the serpentine *S* of Stetriol were fastened to several of their robes.

The sight of them all made Abeke aware of how grimy she was from her days at sea, her hair stiff from salt and her cloak dulled by rain. She wanted a bath, a bed, a night's rest.

"Do you suddenly feel like we've done something wrong?" whispered Rollan, eyeing the Stetriolans' poise, the Greencloaks' stiff shoulders and high heads. They did have an almost military appearance, their backs to the growing crowd, their eyes trained on the ship.

But when the plank was lowered and Abeke and Rollan descended on the dock, two of the Greencloaks stepped forward and smiled.

"Abeke of Nilo," announced the broad-shouldered man with the lemur on his shoulder. "Bond of Uraza."

"Rollan of Amaya," announced the other, a woman who looked like she could have taken the first in a fight. A tattoo of salamander curled around her neck. "Bond of Essix."

As if on cue, the gyrfalcon screeched overhead, before sweeping down to land majestically on Rollan's shoulder.

The crowd gasped and cheered with approval, even though Abeke doubted the stunt was planned. Essix just liked to show off. *A bit like her human*, thought Abeke as Rollan preened.

She thought of summoning Uraza for the same effect (even though the leopard was more intimidating than the falcon), but something caught her eye.

A flash of red in the crowd, not burnt brick or dusty orange, but *crimson*.

Her heart started to race, and she glanced at Rollan to see if he had noticed. But it must have been a trick of the light, because when she looked again, the slice of red was gone.

"Stetriol welcomes such honored guests," said one of the men in blue and black, a lean figure with a trimmed goatee. "If you'll follow us . . ."

Abeke was glad to be back on land.

The crowd parted around them as they passed. Rollan was tense beside her, but even his eyes were wide at the sight of Stetriol—not only the city's appearance, but the *air*. There was a new energy here. In their brief journey through the region before, Stetriol had felt a bit like clothes weighed down by rain. Now, there was a lightness, a buoyancy. Abeke wanted to take in all the changes, but the procession pressed on too fast. Her glimpses of the city were too fleeting.

But even in fleeting glimpses, the change was startling. The Greencloaks had obviously helped import supplies, because everywhere she looked, she saw new construction, old buildings being repaired and new ones being raised. And it wasn't just the buildings. Everywhere she looked, the kingdom was *flowering*. From the potted plants on sills to the lilies floating in the squares' fountains, to the vines climbing the stone walls of courtyards. It looked like a city waking from a long sleep, and Abeke was happy to see it thrive.

For so long, Stetriol had been a place of sickness and anger.

And as easy as it was to hate the kingdom and the Conquerors for what they'd done, Abeke couldn't blame them for doing it. The First Devourer War was many years ago, but its aftermath had stretched on, forcing people to pay for the crimes of their ancestors. Erdas had isolated Stetriol, kept from them the Nectar, let their people suffer bonding sickness and the desperation it brought with it.

People in that position had only two options: die, or fight back.

Could she blame them, for wanting to survive?

If the strain on her bond with Uraza was anything like the sickness the children of Stetriol had felt, could she blame them for wanting a cure?

Not that she could say any of that to Rollan.

Not when Rollan had nearly lost his mother to the Conquerors' Bile.

Not when Abeke had been the one to first trust Shane.

But she wanted to move forward.

"Where are we going?" asked Abeke as the docks fell away behind them and the streets passed in a blur.

The Greencloak ahead of her—the woman with the salamander tattoo—glanced back. "To the castle," she said.

"The castle?" asked Abeke, startled. Stetriol was a kingdom, of course, but it was one without a king. The throne—*Shane's* throne—sat empty.

"The Greencloaks have taken up post in the castle," explained the broad-shouldered man with the lemur, whose name was Bern, "since it is currently . . . unoccupied."

"We share it with the Council of Stetriol," added the woman, Ela. "One of whom, Ernol, greeted you on the docks." She nodded at the slim man with the goatee who was now part of their procession. "It was part of the agreement for rebuilding this city."

"So Shane is no longer the rightful king?" asked Abeke, earning herself a warning glance from Rollan.

"Shane is a fugitive," countered the councilman, Ernol. "He is not *here*, and in the absence of a king, rightful or not, order must be maintained. The royal family did not have the best reputation when it came to diplomacy. But this is a promising direction."

The castle loomed ahead of them, and trumpets sounded as the gates fell open onto a bustling courtyard. Essix bristled at the noise and took wing. Their procession dissolved, half the Greencloaks peeling away to other tasks, along with several of the locals.

"Which Great Beast do you think was summoned?" asked Rollan as they crossed the courtyard, ushered on by the pared-down huddle of green and blue cloaks. "I'm betting Mulop the Octopus. Or maybe Cabaro the Lion."

Abeke hoisted her satchel higher on her shoulder. "I think we're about to find out."

The castle sat on a rise in the middle of the city. Abeke paused at the top of the steps and turned to look out at Stetriol. From here she could see the sweep of tiled roofs, the maze of streets, and, in the distance, *trees*. Along a battered stretch of the city—the buildings reduced to rubble and scorched earth—they'd cleared away the damage and planted trees. Young saplings, none above her knee, but she watched men and women, some in green and others in brown and blue and yellow, planting row upon row of trees.

Abeke's spirits rose at the sight of Greencloaks and locals working together, at the sight of the new growth, and she turned to tell Rollan. But he wasn't there.

The rest of the procession had already gone in, and she found Rollan standing in the castle's entry hall, staring up at a portrait on the wall. Most of the old decorations had been cleared away, exposing the bare stone beneath, but the portrait hung there, one of the only relics of the past.

In it, a girl sat proudly in a chair, a boy at her shoulder. They had the same blond hair, the same sharp eyes, and Abeke recognized them instantly. Even without her Bile-bonded spider, Iskos, Abeke knew the girl was Drina. Royal. *Conqueror*. And Shane's older sister. Shane himself stood at Drina's shoulder, his painted blue eyes looking down at Abeke.

"Why is this still up?" asked Rollan, an edge in his voice.

"A reminder," said Bern. "It doesn't do to pretend the past didn't happen. We can't erase it. We can only try to overcome it."

With that, they were led through the castle halls to a grand room, where a girl was perched on a chair, reading a book, as if she were sitting alone in a library and not on display in a castle. Men and women in blue and black Stetriolan robes—each with the *S* pin of the council—gathered around her as if she were a work of art, a priceless artifact. She looked up when they came in, closed her book, and smiled. The brightness of her smile was matched only by her halo of white-blond hair, which was wound around her head in a braid. Her eyes were sapphire blue, and there was something about the girl that reminded Abeke of Conor—of the way he radiated warmth.

"This is Tasha," said Ernol, going to stand at the girl's shoulder.

"Hello," she said brightly, sitting forward. "You must be Abeke, the brave," she added with a nod. "And you must be Rollan, the fierce." Rollan puffed up at the title, and Abeke almost snorted with laughter. "I've heard so much about you both."

She rose from the chair, looking picturesque, graceful. Right up until she took a step forward and tripped on the corner of her own skirt. The girl gasped and stumbled, knocking into a table with a glass vase before one of the Stetriolan nobles shot a hand out to steady her. None of the councilmembers were fast enough to save the vase, but Bern's lemur appeared, catching the glass before it hit the floor.

Tasha straightened and flashed a shy, embarrassed smile. "Sorry," she whispered.

"Definitely Mulop," whispered Rollan.

Abeke elbowed him in the side.

"Tasha," said Ernol patiently. "Will you show our guests your spirit animal?"

The girl nodded and slid up her sleeve to reveal her tattoo. Abeke's breath caught. Running the length of Tasha's forearm was a swan, its wings spread, as if about to land, or about to rise. Its long, elegant neck was curved into an *S*.

And then, in a flash of light, the mark was gone, its white feathers glowing in the light.

Ninani the Swan.

A reverent silence fell over the room as the Greencloaks bowed their heads and the Stetriolans brought their hands to their chests in reverence.

"No way," whispered Rollan.

The girls' parents—they had the same startlingly light hair, the same bright eyes—stood behind Tasha's chair. Both watched their daughter with pride, and an awe bordering on fear.

It was a sentiment Abeke didn't wholly understand. Her own father had not been happy when she'd summoned Uraza. He'd seen her gift—and the responsibility that came with it—as a burden on him and his village. Abeke had eventually come to terms with her family, but she knew she'd never see such a look in her father's eyes.

Tasha's face, however, was an open book, showing only joy. And why shouldn't she be happy? Summoning a spirit animal in Stetriol had for so long been a curse, the bonding sickness driving its victims mad. It was only recently a blessing, and a rare one.

And Tasha had not only summoned a spirit animal, but a Great Beast.

And not just any Great Beast, but *Ninani*.

The giver of Nectar, so long withheld from Stetriol. It was a symbol of new beginnings. How could they see it any other way?

The swan craned her head and considered her audience with stately grace, her onyx eyes settling on Abeke and Rollan. And then, in a flash of light, she was gone again, returned to Tasha's fair skin as an elegant pattern of feathers and the S-curve of a swan's neck.

The gathered men and women, nobles and Greencloaks, stood for a moment in silence. And then Rollan spoke.

"How many know?" he asked.

"We have kept it secret," said the Greencloak, Bern, at the same moment the Stetriolan councilman, Ernol, said, "Word is spreading."

Abeke's stomach turned as the two men looked at each other, horrified.

"How many have you told?" snapped Bern.

"The city deserves to know," retorted Ernol.

"We told you it *wasn't safe—*"

"We haven't gone shouting it through the streets—" cut in one of the other nobles.

"But the people *will* find out," insisted Ernol, "whether we tell them or not." Abeke watched the volley of words, and then looked at Tasha, who stood between them, confused.

"Then let them find out after she's *safely away*," said Bern.

"Away?" Tasha finally cut in, eyes wide with distress. Abeke realized with horror that the girl didn't know she was in danger, didn't know they'd come to take her back to Greenhaven. Away from her home, from her family, from her world. She'd only just discovered the joys of summoning a Great Beast.

She'd yet to learn the cost.

"Tasha," said Abeke gently, stepping forward. "You cannot stay here."

The girl's smile wavered. "What do you mean? This is my home."

"It's not safe here," added Rollan.

Ernol bristled. "Stetriol is—"

"This has nothing to do with Stetriol," cut in Rollan. "Zerif is hunting down all those who summon the Great Beasts. Once he learns you have Ninani, he will come. We've already lost too many allies—too many friends—to his attacks. We've come to take you with us, back to Greenhaven."

"Such a gift comes to our country," said one of the nobles, "and you want to take it away?"

"We want to protect all of Erdas!" snapped Rollan. A rumble went through the gathered men and women at that. For a very long time, Erdas had disowned Stetriol. "The Great Beasts may bond with one person," he continued, "but they don't belong to one nation."

"We cannot force you to come with us," said Abeke, her attention still focused on Tasha, "but staying here is not only a danger to yourself, but to your city. Plus, you belong with us. Your strength is needed."

Though the news clearly took the girl by surprise, to her credit, she didn't cry. She looked around the room, from the Stetriolan nobles to the gathered Greencloaks to her parents. Her mouth opened, and then closed. "Can

I . . ." she started, stopped, began again, "can I have some time to think?"

Abeke and Rollan exchanged looks, but Bern spoke up. "It will take two days to get the ship restocked and set for sail."

Tasha swallowed and sank back into her chair. She seemed so young, caught between the Greencloaks on one side and the Stetriolans on the other. Ninani may be all grace, but Tasha was all limbs, sharp elbows and bony knees, stretched out in a way she clearly hadn't grown into yet.

"Then I have two days to decide," she said. Rollan looked about to argue, but Abeke caught his arm. They could not force the matter. It had to be her choice.

Ernol spoke up, stepping in front of Tasha. "No one is going anywhere today." Behind him, she saw Tasha's family fold like wings around the girl. "You both must be weary," he said, addressing Abeke and Rollan. "Come, let me show you to your rooms."

Abeke sat in a large tub, scrubbing the salt and sea grime from her skin and wondering what they were supposed to do if Tasha refused to go with them to Greenhaven. When she was done—with the bathing, not the wondering—she found her own cloak was gone. A fresh one, dazzling green, lay folded on her bed. A tray of hot food sat on the table beside it, and Abeke wondered if this was what it felt like to be a royal. She took an apple from the tray, its skin the vivid green of fresh grass.

She and Rollan had both been given elegant rooms in the southern wing of the castle—the castle itself had been divided into north, south, east, and west. The Greencloaks occupied the north and south wings, while the members of the council, a few noble families, and what was left of the royals (a few cousins of Shane's family, mostly), took the east and west. It was strange, thought Abeke, that no one had tried to claim the throne in Shane's absence. Even though Bern had said it was a relic, what with the council in power, she couldn't help but feel like they'd left it empty on purpose. As if they were waiting for their young king to come home.

Abeke leaned her elbows on the window. Her room looked out not onto the city but into the castle grounds and a garden far below. Feeling suddenly restless, she decided to go exploring, in the hopes that a walk through the grounds would do more to clear her head than the bath had.

The sun was setting as she made her way down the stairs toward the gardens. She was nearly there, her mouth full of tart apple, when she almost collided with a boy.

The sight of him made her choke.

The boy—a noble, judging by his clothes—could have been Shane's younger brother. He had the same fair hair, the same slight build, the same intense eyes. The only difference was his mouth. Where Shane's had so often drawn into a smile, especially in those early days—they were, after all, friends before they were enemies—the boy's mouth was a stern line, his eyes hawkish and sharp.

And he wasn't alone.

A small ginger cat, little bigger than a kitten, danced around the boy's legs. Abeke could tell—maybe by the boy's feline grace, or the way they moved in sync—that they were bonded.

Without the Nectar or the Bile, children were bonding naturally. It was becoming even rarer to have a spirit animal, but Stetriol was no longer cut off from the gift.

"Sorry," mumbled the boy, eyes darting over her cloak and face and skin.

"It's okay," said Abeke. "What's your name?"

"James," said the boy.

"And this?" asked Abeke, crouching. "Is she your spirit animal?"

"He," corrected the boy, "is Barnabas."

"Hello, Barnabas," said Abeke, scratching the kitten's ears. He purred against her palm.

"Do *you* have a spirit animal?" asked James, though the green of her cloak meant she obviously did.

"Maybe," she said with a crooked smile.

"Let me see," said the boy imperiously.

Abeke grinned, and then released Uraza.

The boy had the decency to look surprised, staggering back as the massive golden leopard sprang into being, paws landing heavily on the stone floor. James's mouth fell into an O as the big cat, who was nearly as tall as he was, yawned, exposing long, sharp teeth.

When Uraza bowed her head to consider the tiny cat, Barnabas had the audacity to swat a small paw at the leopard's face. It was roughly the size of her nostril. Uraza watched patiently, even tolerating the cat's tinny meow, before she finally opened her mouth and plucked the ginger cat up by his scruff.

Barnabas swung indignantly from Uraza's teeth, and the boy stamped his foot and ordered that the leopard put him down *at once.*

Uraza glanced at Abeke, an amused glint in her violet eyes. Then she dropped the ginger kitten with a plunk and padded away toward the grounds.

Abeke rushed after, trailing the leopard through an archway and into the castle gardens. They were larger than they looked from above, filled with the kind of maze-like greenery that swallowed you up, got you turned around.

Abeke strolled while the setting sun drew long shadows, and the sounds of the castle and the city beyond began to shift, soften.

There was something wild about this place. She could tell that the gardens had once been groomed, but they'd long overgrown their boundaries. Hedges and low divides interrupted the greens. Some were ordinary bushes, but others were strange, bulbous things. She reached out to touch the nearest bush and was surprised when her fingers went through the layer of leaves and into something beneath.

When she pulled aside the viney cover, she realized it wasn't a dense plant at all, but a layer of ivy covering the remains of a cage, the old iron warped and broken and swallowed up by green. Abeke glanced around the garden.

How many of these hedges held other things?

Bern's green-eyed lemur sat on a windowsill halfway up the garden wall, and Essix soared in broad circles overhead. Uraza was obviously happy to be free, and began to prowl around the garden, startling anyone she came across. A noble gave a cry of surprise, and Abeke called the cat back toward her. Uraza didn't come, but Abeke could hear her still prowling through the greenery, hunting small game. Hopefully no one had summoned any small woodland creatures and left them to wander the gardens. When the cat finally reappeared, Abeke was relieved to see that her mouth and paws were clean.

Abeke yawned. She didn't realize it was getting dark, not until the sun dipped behind the castle walls, plunging the courtyard into an early twilight.

She was just about head inside when something caught her attention.

Her senses prickled, the way they did when she was being watched.

Abeke scanned the darkening grounds, and then Uraza let out a low growl, and Abeke's eyes tracked up the garden wall and landed on the figure perched on top. He stood, leaning almost lazily against the place where the garden wall met the side of the castle. He'd be hard to notice in the fading light, but Abeke felt her eyes focus with Uraza's keen sight. She could see him clearly, from the sweep of his red cloak to the silvery wood of his featureless mask.

The last time they'd crossed paths, it had been in the middle of a battle, all chaos.

Now, the world was still.

They stood there, staring at one another, her conversation with Olvan echoing in her head.

He helped us.

Yet he conceals his face.

There was something so . . . familiar about the figure. Which was impossible, she knew. He was covered head to toe, every inch hidden from view except the faintest glint of pale eyes, and in them, recognition.

Abeke opened her mouth, but the boy held a finger to the lips of his mask. A second later she heard Rollan's voice from the archway at the edge of the garden, calling her inside. She heard his steps coming down the path and looked away, only for an instant, but by the time she glanced back at the wall, the stranger was gone.

THE ARACHANE FIELDS

"THERE'S A SAYING AT MY MONASTERY," SAID TAKODA AS they made their way down the path on the right. "It goes, 'There are no easy roads in life. There are no hard ones either. There are only the paths we choose to take, and the places they lead us.'"

"Oh, yeah?" countered Meilin. "What about when you choose one path, but it's full of white-eyed monsters and so you have to double back and take the other road? Is there a saying about that?"

Takoda winced. Meilin knew she was being harsh, but they'd been traveling down the second path for more than an hour, nerves tightening with every passing moment. They'd yet to come upon more of the Many, or a cyrix nest, or anything else that might want to eat them, but Xanthe's warning at the entryway had them all a bit wound up.

All except for Kovo, who lumbered along with his usual impassive glare. But when it was obvious that Meilin had hurt Takoda's feelings, the ape signed a word that she didn't know. She wouldn't have paid it much attention, if he hadn't signed this word at her *several times* so far on their trip—pulling his hand in a gesture over his face.

Finally she asked Takoda to translate. The boy shuffled his feet.

"Um . . ." he said. "It means 'cranky.'"

Xanthe cracked a laugh, and Meilin felt her face go hot. "I'm sorry, the ape who got us trapped under the world is calling me *cranky*?"

In response, Kovo's red eyes found hers. He made the gesture again, slowly enough for her to follow. Meilin raised her staff. Kovo bared his teeth. Takoda chuckled.

"He doesn't mean anything by it," said the boy, waving his hands. "I think he might just be using it as your name."

"My name," growled Meilin, "is not *Cranky*. It's *Mei-lin*."

"If it's any consolation," offered Takoda, "he calls Xanthe *Pale Girl*." The monk ran two fingers along his forearm to show the sign for *pale girl*.

"That's because she *is* a pale girl!" snapped Meilin. "What does he call *you*? Skinny monk?"

"Um . . ." Takoda hesitated, looking to the ape. "Nothing, really. Most of the time he just shoves me."

Kovo lifted his massive hands and Takoda flinched, as if bracing for another shove, but the ape didn't push him. Instead he brought his furry hands up before his red eyes and linked his two forefingers.

Even in the flickering torchlight, Meilin could see Takoda go red.

"What?" she prompted. "What does that mean?"

Takoda smiled shyly. "It means 'friend,'" he translated. Adding, as Kovo made another gesture, "*'little* friend.'"

Xanthe broke into a warm grin. "Aw, that's sweet."

But Meilin rolled her eyes. "Oh, of course," she said, "you get the nice name."

Takoda wasn't paying attention. He was busy signing back to Kovo, linking his fingers, then spreading his arms wide. *Big friend.*

"What does he call me?" asked Conor, his voice soft.

Takoda shot a look at Kovo. The ape hesitated, then curled his hand into a fist, pressed it to his throat, and drew the fist down toward his stomach.

"What does that mean?" asked Conor when Takoda didn't translate.

"Cursed," whispered the boy at last.

Conor swallowed. "Oh."

Briggan growled at the ape. Kovo didn't even flinch.

"Do you hear that?" asked Xanthe. At first Meilin thought the girl was just trying to break the tension, but then she listened and heard it, too. The sound was almost musical, like wind chimes, or the faint plucking of harp strings.

"What *is* that?" she asked, entranced.

"I don't know," said Xanthe honestly.

"Well," said Conor, "we're going to find out."

Up ahead, the tunnel path became narrow and steep, the ground plunging away every few feet, as if they were descending a set of massive stone stairs, each half as tall as Meilin herself.

At the bottom of the steps there stood a kind of archway set into the rock wall. It was made of pale stone, only instead of two limbs, it had seven. It looked like at some point there had been eight, but one had crumbled away with time, and lay in broken pieces on the ground. The archway reminded Meilin of a weeping willow without a trunk, or—she thought with a chill—of the cage of roots in her dream.

Conor was the first one to step through the gateway—Meilin didn't know if it was because he was tired of being coddled, or annoyed by Kovo's nickname, or simply in a hurry to keep moving. As he passed Xanthe, Meilin saw the girl recoil slightly. Meilin glared, and when Xanthe's pink eyes met hers, Xanthe had the decency to look down, ashamed.

Then Meilin heard Conor catch his breath and rushed through the doorway after him, expecting something horrible.

Instead, as she saw what he saw, her mouth fell open in wonder.

One by one, the others followed, and for a moment they all stood there, staring at the world they'd found beneath the earth.

Meilin had seen tunnels and caves and even the sprawling city of Phos Astos. She'd dreamed about the vaulting space beneath the Evertree. But so far, she'd never seen any place like this. The chamber was so vast, she forgot they were underground at all. It didn't seem possible, when the opening stretched so wide she couldn't see the walls, so high the roots and rock were lost in darkness.

So much of Sadre had been harsh edges and sharp stone, like the toothy rocks in the cavern with the Many. But here, everything was softness. Silvery curtains spilled down from somewhere high overhead, and though they were standing on a stone ledge, the floor ahead was covered with delicate strands of light. An intricate network of lines, each shimmering with their own glow. Fields of silvery thread.

The music reached them now, clear as bells, and yet still somehow distant, as if the instrument weren't somewhere in the chamber before them, but all around, everywhere at once. And then Meilin realized that it *was*.

Because the fields themselves were singing.

A breeze blew through the chamber and strummed across the thousands of strings. Their vibrations drew out a faint but steady hum. The sound was eerie and enchanting. Meilin stood there, mesmerized and confused, because she didn't understand what she was looking at, how the floor could make music, how it could be so strange and beautiful. Less like earth than a thousand filaments of light. Like tiny rivers sparkling in the dark floor.

And then she understood.

They weren't lines of water set into the ground.

There wasn't even a ground to be set into.

The threads running together *were* the ground. Or rather, they were a *net*.

Like the nets in Phos Astos, the ones that caught them when they jumped.

But there were no currents of air to guide them, and the net was suspended over a hole so vast and deep it plummeted away into nothing.

And besides, what was a net doing here, in the middle of a cavern without any people?

And then Meilin's stomach turned. Because this net wasn't a net at all.

It was a *web*.

Meilin felt the color drain from her face. Beside her, Xanthe drew in a breath, but she didn't sound scared. Her pink eyes were wide with wonder.

"I know where we are," she whispered. "These are the Arachane Fields."

As if on cue, dozens of small forms as big as Meilin's hand began to crawl up through the spaces between the silver threads. Their bodies glittered like jewels, and their legs—all eight of them—were as spindly as the silk they moved over.

Spider silk.

Meilin looked back at the arch they'd come through. Of course. It had eight legs. She swallowed. She wasn't afraid of many things. Not the dark, not even being buried alive—which was good, considering her current position—but she *did not like spiders*.

She felt herself backing away, retreating until her shoulders came up against something large and warm and covered in coarse hair. A low growl rumbled through the barricade behind her, and she craned her head to see Kovo's fangs. She scrambled forward, her foot nearly skimming the edge of the web.

"I've heard legends about this place," continued Xanthe, almost reverently. Meilin couldn't help but imagine what Rollan would say to that. Probably that legends were rarely told about happy places where nothing bad happened.

As if on cue, Conor said, "Good legends? The kind where everyone lives?"

Xanthe didn't answer that. Instead she said, "The legends say that the Arachane Fields are one of the three wards of protection around the Evertree. Their music is meant to guard the way against evil."

"And the spiders?" whispered Meilin.

Xanthe swallowed. "Well, if I had to guess, I'd say they're meant to catch anything the music doesn't. But as long as we're careful, they should let us pass."

"Should . . ." echoed Conor.

"You said there were *three* wards of protection," added Takoda, whose eyes were fixed on the field.

Xanthe nodded. "The Arachane Fields guard the passage to the Sulfur Sea, and the Sulfur Sea runs like a moat around the Evertree. Beyond the sea . . . Well, the legends get kind of murky, but—"

"One obstacle at a time," said Conor, straightening. "Once we get across the fields, we'll face the rest." Briggan stood tall beside him, ears back but head high, blue eyes trained on the fields ahead.

"There must be another way," said Meilin, trying to keep the fear from her voice.

But Xanthe was already shaking her head. "There was another way, remember? It was filled with the Many."

Meilin swallowed. She would rather take on a hundred of the Many than do this. She thought about suggesting it, but Conor's fevered eyes and Xanthe's set jaw made her hold her tongue.

Meilin's stomach turned over as she scanned the expanse of threads, searching for an edge, some way around, and finding none. But then she noticed that here and there the threads wove together into plats. They weren't as wide as footpaths, but they should hold the weight of four kids. Maybe even Briggan.

But there was *no way* the field would hold the weight of a massive ape.

Everyone seemed to reach the conclusion at the same time, because they turned back toward Kovo.

"Please," said Takoda, linking his fingers in the sign for friend. Meilin had only seen the ape agree to take the passive form once, and he hadn't been happy about it. Now his red eyes tracked over the field. Even the ape must have seen the predicament, because he snorted and brought his heavy hands down onto Takoda's narrow shoulders, and in a flash of light, Kovo vanished, becoming a massive black tattoo that circled the boy's neck and crept across his face. Meilin took a deep breath. The air felt lighter without the ape's looming presence and weighted gaze.

Not that Kovo was the biggest of their problems right now.

Which was saying something.

Conor turned to Briggan, obviously wondering if he should invite the wolf into his passive form, but he hesitated. Boy and wolf met each other's gazes for several long seconds. While Meilin didn't know what passed between them, she saw Conor's hand go to his shoulder, where the parasite was making its slow advance. Was he trying to protect Briggan from the disease? Or to protect the rest of them from *him*?

Whatever it was, the two seemed to reach a silent agreement, because Briggan and Conor looked away at the same time. "Let's go," he said, starting toward the edge.

Meilin was right behind him. Xanthe reached out and took Takoda's hand. She squeezed it, and he squeezed back, and neither one let go.

"Stick to the heaviest ropes," Xanthe whispered to them all. "And watch out for the Webmother."

"What," hissed Meilin, spinning on the girl, "is the Webmother?"

Xanthe managed a nervous smile. "Don't worry," she said. "You'll know her if you see her."

"And if I see her?"

Xanthe bit her lip. "Run."

"Great," said Meilin and Conor at the same time. Even Briggan rumbled. For a long moment, none of them could bring themselves to go. The music played across the field, and the spiders moved along the strings, and it all seemed so delicate. And so dangerous. Like the slightest motion would upset it all.

"Come on," said Xanthe at last, letting go of Takoda's hand. She took a deep breath and set her foot on the thickest strand, testing its weight. It held, and she stepped out onto the cord. The music in the chamber changed ever so slightly with her weight, the resonance shifting a fraction—no, half an octave—lower.

"It's solid," said Xanthe, hands out to her sides for balance.

Takoda went next, taking a strand to Xanthe's right. Briggan sniffed at the cords before padding out onto a third, followed by Conor.

At last, Meilin stepped onto the web. She expected to feel the sickening give of the silk beneath her feet, but it was surprisingly strong. More like metal than cloth. She held her quarterstaff out like an acrobat walking a tightrope, half for balance and half so she had something to look at besides the palm-sized spiders tending the thinner pieces of the web, or the darkness beneath the silver strands.

Darkness that went on and on and on. She couldn't help but feel like, if she dropped something, it would never land.

Don't look down, she told herself. Something the color of rubies skittered to her right. *Don't look at the spiders either.*

She resisted the urge to squeeze her eyes shut. Now, she thought, would be a great time for some of Jhi's calming influence. But it didn't come. Apparently Meilin was on her own.

This isn't so bad, she told herself, and then immediately took it back, remembering a lecture Abeke had given her once about inviting bad luck. *This is bad enough*, she corrected, hoping it wasn't too late. *This is definitely bad enough*.

And yet, somehow, it was beautiful, too. Funny, how things could be both. How the most wonderful places were unsettling, and the most terrifying places possessed a kind of grace.

With every step they made, Xanthe, Takoda, Conor, and Meilin produced a strange sort of music. Xanthe stepped lithely from one strand to another, following the network of strongest lines. As she did, bass gave way to a faint sweet sound. Takoda shifted, and his own tone changed. Briggan padded steadily along. Conor trembled slightly, and the music warbled. Meilin had learned music back in Zhong, in between her lessons in the bow and staff. Now she recognized the trail of keys.

A. C. F.

It was lovely, that music, so lovely that Meilin could almost forget that they were standing on a massive spider-web. Almost.

"In the legends," whispered Xanthe, her words accentuated by the melody, "the spiders tended the Arachane Fields, but they weren't what stopped people from crossing."

A. D. E.

"That was the music," continued Xanthe. "It was said to trap anyone without purpose. To ensnare those with darkness in their hearts."

To Meilin's right, Conor shivered. She wanted to reach out, to lay a hand on his arm, but he was too far away.

"To drag them under . . ." continued Xanthe. "And—"

"You know," said Meilin, careful to keep her voice even. "Maybe now's not the best time for stories. Let's just get across the field."

But the field showed no signs of ending. It stretched on, as far as she could see, the silver threads vanishing into shadow.

A crimson spider with legs as thin and sharp as needles stood several yards away, its many eyes passing over them as it stitched at the web. *Nice spider*, thought Meilin, feeling queasy. *Good spider.*

They were almost there. One more obstacle down, one more test passed, one step closer to the nightmarish Wyrm at the roots of the Evertree, a foe Meilin could fight, an enemy she could defeat.

They were almost there.

Another spider, this one emerald, shone in the corner of her sight.

She tried to imagine Rollan there beside her, not because it gave her strength, but because the thought of him having to navigate this place was funny. Rollan, who liked to put on such a face, pretend he was tough. He hated spiders. Hated anything that crept and crawled. He said it was because of his time on the streets, but Meilin knew they just made him squeamish. In her mind, he shuddered, and stuck out his tongue, and hopped from foot to foot in disgust, and the image made Meilin smile.

And then she slipped.

She didn't fall—she caught herself on two silky, silvery ropes, breath held and body taut—but the sudden movement, the force of her slip and the weight of her body landing, was enough to send a tremor through the web.

First one cord.

Then four.

Then eight.

Out and out like ripples in a pond, until the entire web seemed to be shuddering, the movements leading away from—and back to—Meilin.

She went still, as if that would stop the web's tremor, and bit the inside of her cheek against the sound of fear trying to claw its way up. To every side, her friends stilled. Conor, Takoda, and Xanthe froze, Briggan lowering into a crouch, as all around, the jewel-toned spiders stopped their work and turned their myriad eyes, following the movement of the web.

Meilin squeezed her eyes shut and cursed herself, cursed her tired body and her straining mind, cursed her fear, and the fact that after everything, *she* would be the one to get them killed. She could feel the web shifting beneath her, could feel the spiders' approach, and she forced herself not to fight, because fighting would only draw more spiders. If she stayed still, if she let them come to her and her alone, the others might still get away.

The cord beneath her dipped slightly under the weight of the approaching spiders, and Meilin held her breath.

And then she felt it, on her shoulder, not a spider's needly limb, but a human hand.

Conor's hand.

"I've got you," he said, and even though his eyes were feverish, his grip was strong.

"Thanks," she said, her voice shaking as she let him help her to her feet.

And Conor smiled that warm, kind smile of his, a smile that the infection couldn't take from him, not yet. "You've been saving me a lot lately," he said. "I figured it was my turn."

She saw the ghost of pain crossing his face, felt the tremor in his touch, but he didn't let go, and neither did she.

12

THE FESTIVAL

WHEN ABEKE WOKE THE NEXT MORNING, IN A FOREIGN bed in a foreign city, the air was thick with a coming storm.

She could feel the weather weighing on her chest, brewing in her lungs, and she wished the rain would just start falling. Waiting for storms was always worse than getting soaked.

But all morning, it didn't come.

The clouds hung low with the promise of rain, and made the day muggy, but the storm held back.

Abeke packed and repacked her satchel, read and reread the note from Olvan saying Conor and Meilin and Takoda were still alive. She was as restless as Uraza, who refused to go back into her passive state, despite frightening half the castle residents and stealing two pheasants from the kitchens. The leopard was stretched at the base of the bed, violet eyes closed but tail flicking side to side.

"Fine, then," said Abeke after an hour of pleading. "You can stay here in this stuffy room while I go off on an adventure." She was halfway to the door when she felt the sudden flare of heat against her skin and saw the fresh black of the tattoo running down her arm.

Abeke shook her head. Stubborn cat.

She went looking for Rollan and found him sitting on the floor of a library with the white-blond girl, Tasha. Essix was perched in the windowsill—maybe even she could feel the coming storm. There was a stack of cards on the floor between Rollan and Tasha, but whatever the game was, they were no longer playing it. They were talking. When Abeke caught the edge of their conversation, she hesitated and hung back, hidden from view. It wasn't eavesdropping, she told herself, since they were a team, and she'd have made Rollan tell her everything later anyway.

". . . my city," Tasha was saying, "my parents."

"Yeah, but your parents didn't summon Ninani," said Rollan. "*You* have to make this choice. And I meant what I said, about the Great Beasts not belonging to one land."

"But Stetriol needs me."

"So do the Greencloaks."

Tasha murmured something Abeke couldn't hear, a sound of uncertainty.

"You know," said Rollan quietly, "I didn't want to be a Greencloak at first. I agreed to help them, sure, but I wouldn't put on the color, not for ages."

"Why not?" asked Tasha.

Rollan hesitated. "It felt like too much," he said at last. "It was easier, safer, not to care. You see, for a long time I didn't have anyone, and then all of a sudden there were these people who wanted me around. Needed my help. Cared what happened to me. It was scary, and I knew that if I let it matter, let myself care too much, then I could mess it up. As long as I didn't commit to them, I couldn't really fail. Couldn't let anyone down."

"What made you change your mind?"

"The people I met," he said.

"But I thought they were what scared you."

"They did," he said, then added with a chuckle, "They still do." And Abeke knew he was thinking about Meilin in particular. "But," he went on, "I guess I realized that it's worth it. Caring about people enough to fight alongside them. Caring about something enough to fight for it. There was a Greencloak named Tarik. He showed me . . ." Rollan's voice faltered. "He showed me it was worth it."

Abeke peered around the corner, saw the sadness in Rollan's usually guarded face.

"Is he back at Greenhaven?" asked Tasha.

Rollan swallowed, shook his head, and Tasha seemed to understand what he was saying, and what he *wasn't*.

"I'm sorry," she said, wrapping her arms around her legs, resting her chin on her knees.

"He was like a father," said Rollan after a moment. "And he fought to protect Erdas. *All* of it."

Tasha's gaze went to the window, to Essix and the storm-laden sky of Stetriol. Abeke pressed her back to the wall and listened.

"It's not easy," said Rollan. "It's scary, and it's dangerous, to stand up for things. But there aren't that many people in this world who can really make a difference, and we can."

"We . . ." she said softly.

"You're one of them. One of *us*. But if you stay here, we can't help you. And you can't help us."

There was a long silence. Abeke bit her lip, and heard Rollan get to his feet. "There's never been a Greencloak from Stetriol," he said. "You'd be the very first."

Abeke heard Rollan walking toward the door, toward *her*, when Tasha said, "Okay."

Rollan's steps paused. "Okay?" he echoed lightly.

"I'll come with you," said Tasha, her voice gaining strength. "I'll do whatever I have to, to protect Stetriol. And the rest of Erdas."

"I'm glad to hear it," he said.

Rollan sounded so serious, so mature, but when he rounded the corner and nearly ran into Abeke, he jumped and let out a mousy squeak that made her bite back a laugh. "Gah!"

Abeke clamped a hand over his mouth and tugged him down the hall.

"Do you always have to *creep* everywhere?" he hissed when they were out of earshot.

"It is my way," she said with a shrug and a gentle grin.

"I'm going to put bells on you when you sleep," muttered Rollan, shoving his hands in his pockets. "So I suppose you heard everything I said?"

He sounded a little embarrassed, even though he had no reason to be.

"Enough to know that Tasha's coming with us," said Abeke lightly as they stepped through the castle doors and down into the courtyard. "Good job."

Rollan scuffed his boot and murmured a yeah-whatever-don't-worry, which was about as close as he got to accepting a compliment. "Ugh." He made a stifled noise. "It's so humid I can *feel the air.*" He dragged his hands back and forth.

Abeke looked up. The clouds were darkening overhead, but still no rain. She bit her lip, trying not to take the roiling sky as an omen. Back home in Okaihee, it wasn't just the bad weather that people worried about. The violent dust storms were dangerous enough, but what scared the villagers was the time before they struck. The longer it took for the storm to break, the worse it would usually be.

Looking up at the churning clouds, she had a bad feeling about this one. Did Stetriol usually get this kind of weather? Or was it another side effect of the sickening Evertree?

Beside her, Rollan was still complaining as he wrangled himself out of his cloak and rolled it under his arm.

"Come on," he said, catching her look. "Don't you ever want to take it off and just be Abeke?"

"I *am* Abeke."

"You know what I mean. Not Greencloak Abeke of Nilo, bond of Uraza!" he said, mimicking Bern's deep booming voice. "Just Abeke," he added, returning to his own. Abeke laughed, but the truth was, she understood. She didn't chafe under the mantle like Rollan did, but she still felt its weight. And besides, the humidity from the coming storm *was* oppressive. She shrugged out of the cloak and folded it over her arm, hiding the mark of Uraza beneath the green fabric.

The two walked beyond the castle gates and into town, looking not like Greencloaks, but ordinary kids.

They didn't have a destination in mind, not at first, and simply wandered the streets. For all their differences, Abeke and Rollan shared a restless streak, born of their upbringings, one tracking and hunting on the Niloan plains, the other scrounging on the streets of Concorba. They both hated sitting still.

Besides, it was nice to take in Stetriol without the procession of guards or the scrutiny of a crowd. Abeke's first impressions held true. The city was definitely rebuilding. Doors and windows were open, and people stood talking on steps and picnicking in courtyards. In one square, she saw a female Greencloak and a local carrying a piece of slate together. In another, an old Greencloak and an even older Stetriolan were deep into a game of stones; the Greencloak's animal, a raccoon, playing its own game with pebbles under the table.

The serpent—once the symbol of Stetriol—still marked many of the stores and streets, carved into lintels and etched into curbs, and yet its green S-like pattern now reminded Abeke of the curve of Ninani's neck.

"See?" She nudged Rollan's shoulder as they walked. "It's not so bad, is it?"

"It's like a different world," admitted Rollan grudgingly. But he was obviously still skeptical; she could see him fingering the hilt of the dagger on his belt, scanning the city for trouble.

And then, as they walked down a road lined with shops, trouble ran right into him.

Not in the form of an attacker or a thug, but a small girl, no higher than his waist, clutching a disk of bread.

She stumbled, scrambling to catch the dropped disk,

while heavy steps rang out on the path. Before Abeke could react, Rollan had the girl tucked behind them, and when the pursuer—a heavyset man in billowing blue robes—appeared, demanding to know if they'd seen a thief, Rollan simply shrugged and said, "Can't help you."

The man turned his sweating face to Abeke. "What about you, girl?"

Abeke shook her head innocently, and the man trudged off, cursing to himself. As soon as he was gone, Rollan swung the terrified girl up into his arms. "There now," he said, his voice gentle, teasing. "The trick is to eat the food *while* you're running off with it. That way, there's no evidence!"

Abeke was always caught off guard by Rollan's streaks of kindness. At first she'd pegged *Conor* as the nurturer, but Rollan had a fondness for those in need, and a way with them, too. Within moments he had the girl's tears replaced by a toothy smile, and then a laugh, as he sent her on her way with the disk of bread safely in her hands.

"What?" he said, catching Abeke's look as the girl vanished in the maze of streets.

"I forgot how much you like kids."

Rollan shrugged. "Nothing against kids," he said. "Heck, I'm a kid. It's the grown-ups you have to watch out for." His stomach made a loud growling sound, and he fetched a few Stetriolan coins from his pocket and clinked them in his palm. Olvan had given them some coins before they set out, for necessities, but most of their needs were being met by the castle. Abeke was about to make a joke about them finding some stew when she heard a long, high whistle, followed by a bang.

At first she tensed, assuming they were under attack, but an instant later she saw the burst of purple light against the low clouds, and realized it was a firework.

"Do you hear that?" she asked, craning her head in the direction of the explosion.

Rollan's brows went up. "I think *everyone* heard that, Abeke."

"No," she said. "Not the blast. I mean the *cheering*." She didn't wait for him to answer, but started walking, eyes half-lidded, letting her ears sharpen and pick apart the sounds the way she did when tracking prey. Rollan followed, a stride behind, and as they wound through the city, Abeke could hear the sounds of celebration getting nearer. Shouts and cheers, interrupted by the whistles and pops of smaller fireworks.

All of a sudden they rounded a corner and found themselves at the edge of a growing crowd.

It looked like some kind of festival.

"Oh!" said Rollan, his spirits brightening as he took in the line of stalls. After a moment, his attention narrowed like a hawk, everything else forgotten. "I smell meat."

Another firework exploded overhead, shaking the world like thunder—no, there was thunder there as well, rumbling through the clouds—and the people of Stetriol whistled and whooped. Rollan jogged away, but Abeke couldn't tear her attention from the road, where people were pressing, shoulder to shoulder, jostling to see something around the bend. A procession. When she stretched onto her toes, she could see it rolling down the street toward them.

Men and women in the official blues and blacks of Stetriol waved sticks with bird-shaped kites fluttering on top. It looked like an entire flock. The sticks were a dozen different lengths, the paper birds atop them a dozen shapes and sizes—hawks and eagles, doves and geese—but they'd all been painted white.

Abeke frowned. It didn't make sense. The symbol of Stetriol was a serpent, not a bird.

The air, still thick with impending rain, was now buzzing with excitement, but Abeke's bad feeling was getting worse. "What do you think they're celebrating?" she asked as Rollan reappeared at her elbow with two skewers of what looked like beef.

"Who knows," he said, passing her one of the skewers. "Loosen up. Have a meat stick."

But Abeke waved the food away. Between the brewing storm and the swarming crowd, she was beginning to feel dizzy. The warning plucked at her ribs, and she could almost feel Uraza's coiled energy, her twitching tail, as Abeke's vision sharpened. She scanned the crowd for danger.

Amid the blues and blacks and the fluttering streaks of white, the flash of a red cloak on the other side of the street caught her eye.

"Rollan, look!" she said, tugging on his sleeve. But by the time he turned his attention from his skewer to the crowd, the red had been swallowed up again by the other colors.

"What?" he asked, his mouth full of food.

Abeke shook her head. "I . . . I thought I saw—"

She was cut off by a round of fireworks. The sky lit up with bursts of white. The parade had almost reached them, swelling with every block. Men and women and children cheered as the birds swung and danced on the air.

"Excuse me," said Abeke, touching the sleeve of a woman in front of her. "What is all this for? Is it a holiday?"

"Haven't you heard?" said the woman, twisting toward them. Her face was painted with a swan. "Ninani has come to Stetriol!"

It was like a punch to the stomach.

Rollan cursed beneath his breath. "This isn't good," he said.

"No," muttered Abeke. "It's not."

The arrival of the Great Beast in Stetriol should have stayed a secret. But Ernol was right. Word had obviously spread like fire. Abeke was just wondering *how* when she saw Ernol himself at the center of the crowd, waving a stick with a large white swan fluttering on top.

"That fool," growled Rollan. "He has no idea what he's doing!"

Another firework exploded. Abeke turned and tried to jostle her way through the crowd, swinging the green cloak back over her shoulders. She felt Rollan behind her but didn't look back. They had to get to the castle. They had to find Tasha and Ninani and get away from Stetriol before word spread beyond its borders. Before it reached Zerif.

And then, just as she broke free of the crowd, it hit her.

A wave of sickness.

Suddenly Abeke swayed, feeling ill.

It wasn't the same dizziness that had plagued her through the city with the brewing storm, but a bright, sharp sickness. Her nerves cramped and her muscles twisted around her bones. Pain burned through her, but just as she recognized what was happening and the terror of it hit her, the wave was gone. She could breathe again. She could move. She could think. It had lasted only a second. Long enough to knock the air from her lungs, long enough to make her shake, but even as she trembled, she stared down at her hands, confused. The first time the bonds had strained, the sickness had been much worse. It had seemed to last forever.

Rollan stood beside her, looking pale, his hand bleeding where he'd gripped the skewer too hard and it had broken, cutting into his palm. "Did you feel that?" he mumbled hoarsely. "That was . . ."

Abeke swallowed. "Yeah, but it felt more like an aftershock than an event."

"Yeah," agreed Rollan nervously, "but doesn't an aftershock usually come *after*?"

"Then maybe it wasn't an aftershock," she said, trembling. "Maybe it was a warning."

Rollan opened his mouth, but before he could speak, something caught his attention.

"Hey," he snapped over her head.

Abeke straightened, following his gaze, and saw red. The figure in the red cloak stood several yards away, noticing them as soon as they did him. Again and again he'd looked like a shadow, a ghost, but now he was very real, the ends of his cloak flicking and snapping in the stormy wind. His mask was smooth and empty, but behind it, his eyes were pale and sharp.

He inched back a step, and Abeke held up her hands. "Stop," she said. "We just want to talk."

For an instant, no one moved.

For an instant, she thought he'd stay.

And then a firework went off, shattering any chance of calm.

In the blast of sound and light, the masked boy spun and ran. Rollan growled and Abeke sighed, and the two of them took off at a sprint through the streets of Stetriol.

13

THE CHASE

THE SKY SHUDDERED WITH THUNDER AND LIGHT. The people cheered and sang and crowded in the streets, making it harder and harder to keep sight of the figure in red, let alone catch up to him.

Rollan was starting to wish he hadn't eaten that skewer of meat.

Even with the crimson cloak standing out against the sea of cooler colors, the boy was fast—too fast. He wove through stalls and vanished for long seconds, only to reappear on the other side of a street or on a balcony, climbing a wall or running along the wooden spines of stalls.

The streets of Stetriol were less a grid than a tangled mess, but the stranger moved the way Rollan once had through the streets of Concorba during his years as an urchin, like he knew every crack in the ground, every twist and turn, every way to disappear.

How is he so fast? thought Rollan as they reached the edge of the crowd and swung a hairpin turn. The figure's red cloak had been trailing like a tongue around the corner, but by the time they rounded it, he was gone. Rollan cursed and kicked a bin.

"Split up!" called Abeke, and before he could say that he thought that was a bad idea (because of the crowd and the storm and the fact that he still felt woozy from the weakened bond), she was gone, ducking down another side street in a blur of speed and grace.

"Enough of this," grumbled Rollan, swinging the green cloak back around his shoulders.

He had spent enough time being chased to know the way a person fled when they wanted to lose a tail. He took a running jump, pushing off a stack of empty crates, and then the wall, nearly losing his balance before he caught the tiled edge of the roof and hauled himself up. Lightning forked across the darkening sky, and Essix's screech cut through the air as he clambered up the slate tiles and got to his feet, scanning the streets below. The city unfolded around him, a maze of roads, houses, courtyards, open in a way it hadn't been from the ground. *Sometimes*, thought Rollan, *you just need a change of perspective*. Now, on the roof, he tried to see the city the way he would have back when he was a street thief in Concorba, back before he'd joined the Greencloaks. Before he'd become one of them.

Then again, now that he *was* one of them, Rollan had something he'd never had as a street urchin.

Rollan dropped to a crouch and closed his eyes.

He clutched the tiled roof as the world tipped away, his vision going dark, and then swinging back into focus, no longer on the roof, but overhead.

The change in perspective was dizzying, tunneling in and out with the weakening bond. Again Rollan wished he hadn't eaten that food, but he wasn't about to forfeit the contents on someone's roof, so he tried to focus on Stetriol through Essix's falcon eyes as she scanned the city, searching for a swatch of red.

The celebrations painted the city in bright colors below, sound tangling with light and movement, all so sharp and—

A firework detonated too close to Essix's head, and for an instant Rollan's vision went blinding white. He gasped, gripping the rooftop, but the falcon wasn't wounded, only stunned, and he could feel her annoyance as she dipped and wove through the firework's falling debris. Her vision—now his—returned, and as it did, Rollan saw the shape of the red cloak sprinting away down an alley two blocks south.

"Got you," whispered Rollan, opening his eyes. His sight bottomed out, then settled back into his head. He took a single steadying breath before launching off along the roof's edge, tracing the gutters and climbing the peaks until he caught sight of the red cloak rounding a corner up ahead.

From his vantage point on the roof, Rollan smiled.

The stranger in red must not know the city as well as he thought he did, because he was heading straight into a dead end. The sides of the narrow street were high, and instead of giving way onto another road, the alley turned a corner and ended abruptly in a brick wall, the back of some tavern or inn.

Rollan ran along the rooftops, and then, before the masked figure could realize his mistake, Rollan dropped from the courtyard wall and landed in a crouch before him, blocking the only way out.

"Aha!" he said with a grin. "Caught you."

The figure turned, the silvery wood of his mask eerily smooth and faceless. Up close, there was nothing specter-like about the stranger. He was tall—taller than Rollan, anyway—and Rollan tried not to think about the way his opponent had taken on Suka the Polar Bear.

"Take off that mask," said Rollan, taking a step forward and drawing his dagger. "There's nowhere to go."

He heard steps, and Abeke rounded the corner, skidding to a stop beside him when she saw the masked figure.

"Who are you?" she called out, breathless.

The boy in red didn't speak. He held up his hands, eyes narrowed to slits behind his faceless mask. Rollan didn't know if he was surrendering or telling them both to stay back. Then, in one fluid motion, the figure spun away and leaped, pushing with startling strength off the corner of the wall and vaulting one, two, three steps straight up the wall before landing on top of the roof. He didn't flee. From his new perch the stranger turned to face them again, almost taunting.

"No, you don't!" Rollan tried to follow, took a running start at the wall and jumped. He got one boot up, and almost got two, but before he could manage the second he lost his footing and fell back to the street, landing roughly on his backside. He could have really used Arax's old talisman right about now.

"Okay," he grumbled, getting to his feet. "You can stay up there . . ." Over the stranger's shoulder, he saw Essix diving, talons forward, and smirked. ". . . For all I care . . ."

Essix screeched and sank her nails into the stranger's back. Or at least, she meant to. At the last second the stranger spun, cloak billowing as he dodged Essix's talons and somehow kept his balance on the roof's edge. The falcon tried to bank, but the stranger's hand shot out and caught Essix by the throat.

Rollan let out a panicked sound. Essix tried to claw her way free, but her talons raked uselessly against the stranger's forearm, as if he were wearing armor. The stranger's grip tightened.

"Stop!" cried Rollan, but the figure in red didn't hurt the bird.

"Call her back," he ordered, his voice low and gruff, slightly muffled by the mask.

Rollan didn't hesitate, and neither did the falcon. He called Essix back to him, and Essix came; in a flash of light she vanished from the stranger's hand and reappeared on Rollan's skin. The masked figure turned his head sharply, as if hearing something in the distance. Something besides fireworks and thunder and song.

"Who are you?" demanded Abeke again. The figure's masked face tipped down as he considered her. Another fork of lightning split the sky behind him, and his cloak fluttered ominously in the wind. "Why are you following us?" she added.

When at last the stranger answered, all he said was, "You should go."

"Oh, yeah?" Rollan snapped. "Why don't you come down here and make—"

"Why were you in the forest that day?" cut in Abeke. "And why are you here in Stetriol? Are you trying to collect the Great Beasts for yourself?"

The faceless mask tipped to the side. "No," he said sternly. "We seek to protect the future from the past."

Oh, great, thought Rollan. Now the stranger was talking in the royal *we*.

Again, something caught the masked boy's attention. Something Rollan couldn't see. "It's not safe here," he said. "You need to . . ."

But his words trailed off, swallowed not by a rumble of thunder but by the rushing of blood in Rollan's ears. An instant later, the crushing pain hit him, this time not in a warning, but in a *wall*. He could feel the bones in his body shudder in time with the Evertree as it trembled halfway across the world. Pain—crushing, tearing, lasting pain—tore through his body, and the next thing he knew he was on his hands and knees, trying not to black out.

He heard Abeke scream beside him, heard her small body collapse to the cobbled street. But Rollan couldn't help her, couldn't even call her name. He tried, but his jaw was clenched, teeth locked together in agony as he curled in on himself, something deep inside him twisting so hard he was sure it would break. Rollan's vision swam, and he pressed his palms against his eyelids, trying desperately to make the stuttering vision stop.

And then, at last, he felt it.

A drop of cold rain broke the fevered spell of the tearing bond, dragging him back to his senses. Cold rain kissed his temple, his cheek. Cold rain slicked the ground beneath him and tapped a beat against his arms. Rollan wanted to stay there, curled on the alley floor, and let the rain wash over him until the last of the burning pain was gone. He wanted to, but he couldn't. It felt like hours lost, when it was only minutes, and he had to get up.

Something was wrong. Hadn't something been wrong?

A boy in red. A girl in white. A swan.

Ninani.

Stetriol.

The parade.

This is how his mind came back to him, in drops of rain.

Thunder rolled through, but it sounded too low, too close.

He heard Abeke's shuddering breath beside him, saw her roll onto her stomach, then rise to her knees.

Everything ached, and his heart was pounding in his head, but he could move again, and he forced himself up to his hands and knees.

"You *need to get up*," said a voice gruffly.

Rollan looked up. He'd expected the masked boy to be long gone, or at least atop the wall, but he was standing in the alley, masked face bowed over Rollan, boot prodding his shin. "Get. Up."

"Who do you think you are?" snapped Rollan, staggering to his feet, his body still ringing with pain.

"You need to go *now*," said the figure in the red cloak. "They're coming. They were waiting for you to stumble. Now they're here."

"What are you talking ab—" started Abeke, but she was cut off by an explosion.

Another firework, only this one wasn't overhead.

The boom seemed to come from the top of a building nearby, and Rollan's stomach turned as it was followed an instant later by a scream of terror, the rain of slate tiles crashing to the ground.

Why had someone shot off a firework so low?

In his dazed state, it took Rollan a moment to understand.

Stetriol wasn't celebrating anymore.

The city was under attack.

UP IN FLAMES

CONOR WASN'T AFRAID OF SPIDERS, AND EVEN IF HE WAS, they were the least of his problems right now.

The group was halfway across the Arachane Fields when his hands started to shake again, and his vision tunneled, and the whispers began to weave through the music in his head. He was getting too tired too fast. He might actually have told Meilin that he needed to stop, needed a break to collect his energy, his thoughts, if they weren't standing rather precariously in the middle of a sprawling spiderweb.

A strand away, Meilin made her way cautiously forward, along with Xanthe and Takoda.

Conor took a step and nearly missed the silver thread entirely when his vision doubled at the last instant. His breath caught as he fought for balance. The web trembled beneath him, and the nearest spider, its body amber and its limbs black, pivoted to look at him with its many, many, many eyes. Conor felt in that moment as if it could see the darkness roiling inside him.

The Arachane Fields . . . guard the way against evil.
And the spiders?
. . . catch anything the music doesn't.

Conor swallowed. The spider chittered, and he could *feel* the parasite moving beneath his skin. But the more he thought about it, the more the spiders in the web seemed to think about *him*, so he wrestled with his panic and fear, tried to find calm the way he had so long ago, when he was only a shepherd tending a flock in Trunswick. How many hours had he spent there, gazing up at the sky, finding peace in the slow procession of clouds, the steady blue, or even the soothing sound of rain?

He tipped his head back now, the way he had then, only to be reminded that there was no sky here, clear or stormy. There was only the ceiling of the cave, so high above it vanished into black.

"Conor?" came Meilin's voice, over the whispers and the field's strange melody. That voice was the closest thing he had to a sky—not a stretch of blue, but the steady slate gray of a winter afternoon—and he held fast to it. And when Briggan rested his muzzle against his back, Conor grounded himself in that, too. In the simple weight of a friend's voice and a familiar's steadfast calm.

He took a deep breath and continued forward, steady, steady.

And then, just as he was stepping from one strand to another, he felt it. Like a blow to the chest, all the air knocked out of him in a sudden burst of pain. At first he thought it was the parasite, clawing through his nerves, but then he saw Takoda gasp and bow his head, saw Meilin stop and clutch her chest, and realized that whatever it was, they could feel it, too, which meant it could be only one thing.

The bond.

Briggan cowered beside him with a whine, and Conor forced his body down into a crouch to keep from toppling over into the dark, bracing himself for the spine-curling agony that had hit him once before.

But it didn't come.

In fact, almost as quickly as the pain shuddered through him, it was gone. A passing shadow, a glancing blow.

"What was that?" asked Xanthe, pink eyes wide with confusion. "What happened to you guys?"

"The bonds," hissed Takoda through gritted teeth. "Our spirit animals . . . the tree . . ."

"That wasn't . . . so bad," gasped Conor, still on his hands and knees.

"It doesn't make sense," said Meilin, rubbing her chest. "The Evertree is getting worse, not better. The effects of the strain should be getting worse, too."

"Maybe," said Conor, trying to suppress the waver in his voice. "But you won't find me complaining. If I never feel that again, it'll be too soon."

He straightened and realized with surprise and dread that the web beneath them was no longer flat, but bowing heavily under a new weight.

Conor looked up and tensed with horror as he saw Kovo standing among them.

Takoda had either summoned the Great Beast, or the ape had been released with the shuddering of the bond. It didn't matter. All that mattered was that the massive ape was now standing in the field of silver thread, and even though the web didn't snap, it warped and bent around Kovo's weight. Realization rippled through the group, but they weren't the only ones.

The spiders around the web had noticed, too.

They clicked and hissed, and began to skitter across the web toward the bowing center.

"Takoda," snapped Meilin, fighting for balance as the ground tilted beneath her. "Put him away!"

"I . . . I can't."

"*Try!*" said Conor.

"Come on, Kovo," said Takoda, voice pleading. The ape only bared his teeth and growled. Briggan snarled back, an alpha trying to subdue a member of his pack, but Kovo was no wolf. He beat his chest and made a sound that shook the strings and sent the melody scattering.

"He's going to break the web!" shouted Meilin as the spiders skittered closer.

"Kovo," insisted Takoda, trying to keep his voice low and even as he pulled open the collar of his robe and exposed his throat, where the mark of the Great Beast had been. "Please."

The ape turned his red eyes on the boy, and for a second Conor thought he might actually, grudgingly, obey.

But then something moved behind one of the curtains of silver thread. They all spun as a creature parted the curtains and stepped through. Briggan bristled, and Kovo clenched his fists, and Conor gaped as out came the largest spider he had *ever* seen. Larger than a spider had any right to be. Its body was as big as Kovo's, its legs as thick as the cords of silver silk they balanced on. A hundred eyes—some emerald and others sapphire and others amber—stared out from its head. Venom dripped from two fanglike pincers that hung below its jaw.

Meilin actually swayed on her feet, the last of the color draining from her face at the sight of the giant arachnid.

The Webmother, thought Conor.

Kovo had disturbed the *Webmother*.

And unlike the smaller spiders that, until Kovo's reappearance, had left them alone, the Webmother hissed and clicked and immediately started toward them.

"Uh-oh," said Xanthe.

Conor craned his head and could just make out the far edge of the field, the place ahead where silver thread gave way to stone again. They needed to run, but there was no way. The Webmother clambered toward them from one direction, and the dozens of smaller spiders were spilling in from every other side, surrounding the group with eyes and legs and chittering. On instinct, Conor tried to retreat, and nearly lost his balance on the thread.

"Xanthe," he said, voice tight. "Anything in the legends about what to do now?"

"No . . ."

"Great," growled Meilin, gripping her staff. "I guess we fight."

"Wait." The pale-skinned girl actually took a step *toward* the Webmother, hands raised as if in supplication. "Maybe we can talk—"

"Do you speak spider?" asked Takoda anxiously.

"No, but if she understands that we just want to—"

The giant spider hissed her disapproval, jaws opening.

"Bad plan," said Meilin, grabbing Xanthe's shoulder and pulling her backward, narrowly avoiding the bead of venom that dripped from the Webmother's fangs. It fell to the silver cords and sizzled.

While Xanthe and Meilin had been struggling before the Webmother, Kovo had been signing something to Takoda, and after a second Conor realized what the gesture meant.

Fire.

Fire, fire, fire, signed the ape with urgency, tugging on Takoda's bag until the boy took out the unlit torch and the flint.

Xanthe spun at the sound of flint striking.

"No, *wait,*" she pleaded, but it was too late. A spark caught the torch's head and lit, burning with reddish-gold light against the field's blue-silver. Takoda held the flame high, and the surrounding spiders scrambled backward in the face of the torch's heat and glow, their many eyes alight. The Webmother reared up at the sight of the fire, screeching in anger and shaking the web beneath them.

Meilin tore a piece of fabric from her shirt and wrapped it around her quarterstaff, touching Takoda's torchlight to the cloth until it caught, too. Takoda faced the Webmother while Meilin swung the quarterstaff back and forth to ward off the smaller spiders, her knuckles white around the wood.

They were surrounded. But the fire seemed to be keeping the spiders at bay.

"Now what?" asked Xanthe.

"We move as a group," said Meilin. "All together, toward the edge of the field." And for a few steps, as they shuffled forward, with spiders circling, backs together across the strongest threads, Conor thought it might actually work.

They were their own beast, a many-limbed, fire-eyed creature, moving carefully, if not gracefully, across the silver web.

And then the Arachane Fields trembled.

A shudder went through the entire cavern, not just the cords of spider silk beneath his feet, but through the vaulting cave above, as the unseen roots of the Evertree tensed and twisted and writhed.

Oh no, thought Conor, just before the pain hit him like a wall.

If the first shudder had been a glancing blow, this was a beating.

The world around him fell away, the Arachane Fields and the silvery light and the spiders vanishing with the rest of Conor's sight as the pain ripped through him. His body tore itself away from his will, collapsing to the web like a puppet with the strings cut. He curled in on himself as every muscle in his body spasmed and every bone ached. Somewhere, Takoda cried out and Kovo roared with fury and beat his chest, Briggan howled, a wild, wolfish cry, and Meilin screamed and fell to her knees. Conor fought the sickness, fought the pain, fought his body the way he'd been fighting it for weeks, and struggled to his hands and knees.

Through the tears streaming down his face, he saw the spiders on the web frozen like drops of dew, their many-eyed faces turned up toward the suffering roots.

He saw Meilin driving the end of the quarterstaff into the silver cord beneath her, trying to force herself up.

He saw Takoda sway on his feet, and Xanthe, the only one of them immune, catch the boy before he fell.

Catch the boy, but not the torch.

Saw it go tumbling to the field of thread.

Saw the web catch instantly, the silver thread lighting like oil.

Conor gasped, clawing his way back to his senses as the fire licked outward, and the Webmother and her kin recoiled, and Briggan—his Briggan—eyes wide in animal horror, took off at a run across the igniting fields.

"Briggan!" shouted Conor, scrambling, stumbling, forcing himself back up as the wolf sprinted away across the silver web, looking less like a Great Beast and more like a spooked dog. All around them, the threads began to melt and snap. The music they'd made, once sweet, now warbled and fell apart like a melody dropped, the chords tripping out of tune and then tumbling away entirely, replaced by the shriek of the spiders and the crackle of flames.

"Conor!" called Meilin, now up on her feet. She stumbled backward as a cord in front of her caught fire, and through the billowing white smoke, he saw her point to the end of the field up ahead. But all Conor could think about was finding Briggan.

He spun, disoriented by the echoes of pain and the rising chaos, the light and heat and smoke, and then with terror he saw the wolf trapped by a fiery curtain, the world around him going up in flames, the web warping around the wolf's paws. Briggan turned in a slow, nervous circle, hackles up, cornered by fire. There was no way back. No way Briggan would ever reach Conor, let alone the edge.

But when he reached out, tried to invite the wolf back into his passive state, Briggan did not come.

A tendril of fire scorched the wolf's tail and he yelped, tried to pad forward, then back, trapped on the unsteady ropes.

"Briggan!" called Conor, pulling on their bond. But it was too weak, and Briggan's blue eyes stayed wild. He was too much wolf right now, too little spirit animal . . . but Conor knew it was more than that. Knew that, deep down, he didn't *want* to let the wolf come back, didn't want to tether Briggan to his failing body, because he was scared of the parasite infecting him, too.

More web fell away. Briggan's paw slipped as the silk cords beneath him melted.

Briggan was trapped, and Conor was terrified, and the world was falling apart around them, but he knew that, whatever monsters he had to face, he couldn't face them without his wolf.

He threw out his hand and pulled on the bond with all his strength.

"BRIGGAN!" he called the Great Beast back.

And, at last, the Great Beast came.

Briggan vanished from the web just before it crumbled underneath him, and in a flash of light and heat he reappeared on Conor's skin, a wolf leaping up the arm opposite his wound.

The wolf's return hit him in a wave of energy and relief. Briggan's wild strength surged through Conor, and he spun and sprinted with a wolf's power and balance toward the edge of the field, the place where the silver net stopped and the ground—solid rock—began again. His vision blurred with smoke and tears, but all he could think of was reaching the ledge.

One loping stride, then two, and he was there across the threshold, coughing and stumbling gratefully off the crumbling web and onto solid stone.

Safe.

And then, just as suddenly, not safe.

Because what he didn't see, not until it was too late, was that the stone ground ended almost as abruptly as it began. The rock was not an expanse but a line, a ridge that gave way suddenly, violently, to nothing. A sheer drop. There was no more ground ahead. No more anything. Conor staggered to a stop on the precipice, so close his toes were curling over the edge, loose pebbles crumbling away and falling down into the dark.

He was the first to reach the rock, and he turned to warn the others, to stop them from barreling forward out of fire and into a fall.

"Wait!" he called as Meilin surged forward onto the ledge, her head down.

Too late.

She looked up at the last minute, her face smudged with ash. She didn't see the chasm, but she saw Conor's panic and tried to pull back in time. But she had too much momentum and too little space. The two of them collided on the precipice.

Conor lost his balance, felt the world give way beneath his feet. For an instant, they both hung there, and then they came apart. Meilin dug in her heels, wrenched herself away. She landed on the stone platform, and Conor was falling back, back, into nothing.

A hand caught his wrist.

It wasn't Meilin's.

It was Xanthe's.

"I've got you," she said, breathless. They both looked at the place where her pale fingers gripped his sleeve. Meilin was on her feet again. She grabbed his other hand and the two hauled Conor upright on the ledge.

Xanthe let go, turning back to the blazing field.

"Be carefu—" she called, but she never had the chance to finish. Takoda and Kovo were barreling forward, the world on fire at their back. Xanthe dove out of the way as the boy and the ape crashed onto the stone ledge, colliding with a force that slammed into Meilin, who slammed into Conor, and suddenly they all went tumbling over the side and into the dark.

15

FALLING

ONE SECOND THEY WERE STANDING ON THE LEDGE, A field on fire at their backs, and the next, they were falling. Meilin didn't know what happened, only that she was holding on to Conor, and then something hit her from behind, and the ground she'd worked so hard to reach was suddenly gone.

And she was plunging down through empty air.

Back in Zhong, she'd always enjoyed the rush of sparring with her tutors, the thrill of a challenge, the way her heart leaped into her throat. She did *not* enjoy the rush of falling. Her heart was still there, in her throat, along with her stomach, and a scream.

Of all the ways to die, this was not the one she had in mind.

But then, too soon, her side hit mud, and suddenly she wasn't falling so much as sliding down a very steep slope covered in mossy earth and slimy stones.

She reached blindly for something, anything, to catch hold of, but couldn't get purchase. Her body had momentum, and she couldn't figure out which way was up long enough to do anything but fall. And then, as suddenly as the world below her had gone from air to mud, it was very briefly air again, and then water.

Meilin broke the surface with a crash, and spluttered and tried to swim before she realized that the water wasn't deep. She was sitting on the silty floor of a pool, or a pond, or a shore. Whatever it was, the water sloshed around her knees as two other bodies thudded into the shallow expanse beside her, followed by a thunderous crash that could only be Kovo.

"Blech," said Conor, spitting out a mouthful of grimy water. And he was right. The liquid tasted even worse than it smelled, and it smelled pretty awful.

What had Xanthe called this place, the obstacle beyond the Arachane Fields?

The Sulfur Sea.

She thought she understood why. The air was damp and rotting, and there was a gritty quality to the water, though that might have been the silt they kicked up with their fall. Still, it looked black and brackish as it slid between her fingers. Meilin squinted, straining to see the space around her. There was no light, except for the distant burning of the fields far overhead. It cast strange shadows over everything, turned the world to black and white. At their back was the cliff they'd just descended. Ahead, nothing but a stretch of oily water, trailing into darkness. Meilin thought, not for the first time, about how much she preferred the world *above* ground.

"Is everyone all right?" asked Conor hoarsely.

Takoda mumbled something affirmative, and Meilin got to her feet, brackish water soaking through her shoes and sluicing off her cloak. She'd lost her quarterstaff in the fall, heard it break halfway down. She plunged her hands back into the gritty water to search for the pieces, but her fingers found only mud, rocks. Her hand slid over something smooth, and then moved against something that moved back.

Meilin recoiled.

She couldn't see through the water. Its surface was a dark slick reflecting only the pale planes of her face and, above, the burning field. Maybe it was best, she thought, even as she forced herself to ask.

"Xanthe," she said, teeth chattering from the damp soaking through her clothes. "What do you know about the Sulfur Sea?"

But Xanthe didn't answer.

"Xanthe?" Meilin said again as something brushed her shoe. "Whatever the legends are, we need to know."

But still the girl didn't speak. Meilin straightened and squinted. In the flickering haze, she could make out the broad shape of Kovo, the narrow one of Takoda, the hunched form of Conor.

No Xanthe.

"Xanthe?" called Conor.

Nothing.

"Xanthe?" called Takoda, voice rising.

Meilin spun in a circle.

There were no pale-skinned bodies floating in the shallows, no girl-shaped shadows standing on the ledge above. Meilin sloshed forward along the shore, heart pounding in her chest. Xanthe knew the way. She was the only one who did.

"Xanthe!" Meilin called out, but she was answered only by her own voice, echoing over the water.

The girl was gone.

ATTACK ON STETRIOL

ABEKE WAS BARELY ON HER FEET WHEN THE BLAST RANG out, far too low for fireworks.

The ground shook with the force of the explosion. The air, once filled with cheers and music, was suddenly overtaken with smoke and screams.

"Get to the castle," ordered the masked figure. "Find the girl. Get her out."

And before Abeke could say anything else, he turned and leaped off the wall, vanishing behind it.

Rollan unleashed Essix, and the falcon went soaring angrily up into the sky.

Abeke's body was still singing with pain, her muscles aching and her thoughts dull, but she managed to mount the wall after the masked boy. His red cloak was already gone, but when she turned to survey what was unfolding across Stetriol, the air caught in her chest. Someone must have set blaze to a toppled supply of fireworks, because another went off, and then another, explosions streaking through the city and colliding with walls, buildings, homes, bursting into flame and light and filling the city with smoke.

Drops of rain hit the ground around her, along with debris—loosened shingles, singed pieces of canvas—but the skies had yet to truly open, and the city was beginning to break and burn.

Figures were swarming through the streets, some human, some animal, their foreheads marked by the horrible black spiral of the infected. Zerif's creatures. They moved in a kind of hive mind, like a murmuration of starlings or a colony of ants, overtaking everyone and everything they reached. At every street some peeled away, fanning out to maximize the damage, but the core was heading straight for the castle.

She strained to find the Greencloaks and saw with horror that half of them were still on their hands and knees, crippled by the latest bond strain. Rollan had been looking past her up at the sky, swaying on his feet as his vision emptied and Essix's dark shape swept overhead. An instant later he was back, looking ill. And she could tell he'd seen the same things.

"This way," he said, his voice tight as Abeke jumped down, landing in a crouch beside him.

They backtracked out of the alley and reached the nearest intersection just as two infected pinned a man down in the street.

Rollan caught Abeke's arm before she could race forward, pulled her back into the shadow of the wall as one of the infected raised a dagger to the man's neck. Instead of striking, a dark shape emerged from his cuff and slid the length of the metal, latching on to the man's throat.

He writhed and spasmed as the parasite crawled beneath his skin, over his jaw, up his cheek. And then, too soon, his fighting stopped. His body went slack and his captors let go, and the next moment he was on his feet again, the spiral pulsing on his brow.

He lunged for the nearest woman—a Greencloak—and Abeke reached for her bow, only to remember it was back at the castle. And then Rollan's knife went whistling through the air and caught the infected man in the hand, buying the Greencloak an extra moment, a chance to get away. Rollan grabbed Abeke's arm as the other two infected turned toward them.

"Come on," he said, pulling her in the direction of the castle. "We can't save everyone, but we have to save Tasha while there's still time."

The streets were full of shouts, but none of them belonged to the infected. That's what unnerved Abeke most, their silence. Their mouths hung slightly open, air rasping between their teeth. But they said nothing, only came with blade and hand and parasite, corrupting all they touched, and killing what they couldn't. And their animals—their *animals*—attacked, their eyes neither keen nor wild, but empty.

Vessels for something else's will.

A dog bit into a woman's leg, a parasite wriggling between its teeth. A marked lizard snaked across the stone. Overhead, a hawk with a black spiral swooped for Essix, but the gyrfalcon was fast and cunning and got away. Nearby, an owl wasn't as lucky.

Please, thought Abeke as they raced toward the castle, *please never force me to see Conor like this.*

They raced down the streets—streets they'd so recently wandered through laughing, now a scene of terror.

Abeke and Rollan got to the castle gates hoping to find allies, but they found only more chaos. An hour before, the courtyard had been a hub of life, locals and Greencloaks working together. Now some fought together, and others grappled, and others still struggled against their own infected friends. The courtyard was a mess of bodies, several of them down, the rest fighting. Spirit animals swooped and charged, the infected waging war against the bonded, who desperately tried to ward them off.

The infected wore an array of colors, but the clothes meant nothing to them now. The fabric hung from their bodies, the collars torn, the cuffs ragged. All thought of who they were—who they'd been—was now lost to the sickness. Some looked like they might have once been criminals while others wore the marks of nobles—but now they were stripped of everything but blind service, enslaved by Zerif. By the Wyrm.

A handful of Greencloaks were trying to hold the front steps, Bern among them.

"We have to find Tasha!" called Rollan, blocking an infected's sword. He kicked the man in the chest and sent him sprawling backward. The infected were strong, but not agile, and it took the man several seconds to stumble to his feet, where a female Greencloak drove a dagger through his back.

"Still inside!" called Bern as he cut down another attacker, his lemur nowhere to be seen. "Find her and go."

Abeke found a cart of weapons inside the courtyard. She took up a quiver and bow just as a woman threw herself ferally at Rollan. Abeke nocked the arrow and loosed it without hesitation; it plunged into the infected's shoulder. But the woman only hissed and dragged the barb free, seemingly oblivious to the blood running down her front.

"Aim for the heart or the head," ordered one of the Greencloaks. "Nothing else will stop them!"

An osprey shrieked and dove for Abeke's face, talons outstretched, only to be taken down by another Greencloak's arrow. But as she turned to thank the archer, the man fell to an infected with a jagged knife.

Rollan surged up ahead, vanishing into the castle, but just as Abeke reached the entrance, a wild dog sprang through. It lunged for Abeke, its pale fur marred by the black spiral above its eyes as it took her down, pinning her against the landing. She dug her hands into its scruff and fought back its snapping jaws, and then in a flash of light Uraza was there. The leopard pounced, tearing off the dog; it went rolling down the steps. Abeke got to her feet and said a breathless thanks before she and Uraza plunged into the castle.

More Greencloaks fighting. More falling. A blond woman, one of the Greencloaks from the *Tellun's Pride II*, was now on her knees, clawing at her throat as a dark shape crawled beneath her skin. Abeke saw the horrible moment when the fighting stopped and the struggle went out of her eyes.

"In here!" called Rollan from up ahead.

They found Tasha in one of the great halls, cornered by enemies. Two women, a man, and a jaguar. The man was a Greencloak, and one of the women a Stetriolan noble, and none of that mattered because all of them bore the mark of the infected on their skin. Tasha's back was up against the wall, a broken chair leg clutched in her hands, and Ninani before her with wings raised into a large white shield.

More steps were coming down the hall. Not the even tread of allies, but the lumbering tread of those already lost. Rollan spun and barred the door, shoving a shelf in front of it.

And even though Abeke knew they couldn't go back out that way, knew the odds would only get worse with the doors open, she still felt trapped. Which, of course, they were.

"Hey!" Rollan called to the attackers cornering Tasha. "Let's even things out!"

Two of the infected turned at the sound of Rollan's voice, but the third was undeterred, still advancing on Tasha and Ninani. She was reaching toward the swan, a black worm in her palm.

It all happened so fast.

Ninani hissed and reared, and Abeke drew her bow and launched an arrow, piercing the woman's hand and knocking the parasite to the floor. Tasha surged past the swan and swung the chair leg as hard as she could, missing the first time, but landing a blow the second time that dropped the woman to the ground, dazed.

"Ha!" said Tasha triumphantly, just before the woman grabbed her foot and sent her sprawling to the floor, chair leg rolling out of her grip.

"I'm sorry, I'm sorry," said Tasha as she tried to scramble away, kicking as the woman crawled toward her, grasping.

Abeke nocked another arrow and loosed it.

Aim for the heart or the head.

The barb found its mark, and the woman fell lifeless to the floor in front of the girl.

Tasha's face flooded with relief, but the fight was far from over.

The jaguar turned its hollow gaze on Uraza, who yowled and leaped forward, the two big cats colliding and going down in a tangle of claws and teeth.

Rollan took on one of the attackers, a woman with stringy black hair, and Abeke faced the other, a lanky teen lifting a knife. They both had loose parasites climbing over their clothes, searching for their next host.

"Don't let them touch you," Abeke told Rollan.

"Don't worry," said Rollan, turning a knife in his hand. "I'm not letting them get close."

He slashed with the knife, but the woman dodged, the movement eerily fast and fluid. Her fingers tangled in his collar and he struggled before clocking her upside the head with the butt of the blade.

"Aaahh," said Rollan, shaking the parasite from his cloak and crushing it underfoot as the lanky man slashed at Abeke. He was too close for her to shoot, and when she brought the bow up to deflect, his knife came down hard, cracking the wood. She swept his legs out from under him, then cracked her boot across his face.

Abeke spun, searching for Uraza. The first thing she saw was the jaguar's body slumped on the ground. And then it shifted, rolled aside, and the leopard dragged herself slowly to her feet. A gash ran along Uraza's shoulder, and when Abeke saw her spirit animal's lumbering step, her heart stopped with fear. But then the leopard dragged her gaze up, and her eyes were clear and violet, with no sign of infection, no parasite. Abeke threw her arms around the leopard, pressing her forehead to the Great Beast's muzzle.

"Not to break up a moment," cut in Rollan as he crossed to the window, "but we need to go. Tasha. Ninani."

The girl was on her feet again. In a flash of light, the swan vanished, reappearing as a pattern of wings and the curve of a neck down Tasha's arm.

On the other side of the room, the doors shook.

Someone was trying to get in. Abeke hesitated, glancing back.

"Come on," he said. "Help me get this window open."

"What if it's Bern?" she asked.

Rollan swallowed. "I don't think it's Bern."

"We should make sure," she pressed.

He looked to the doors. "Bern?" he called out. "Is that you?" There was no answer, only a growl, and the shudder of the doors against the chest. Rollan looked back at Abeke. "Not Bern. Come on."

He put his weight behind the massive latch—the wood swollen from the storm—and Abeke and Tasha joined him. Together they got the metal to turn, and the window swung open.

The great hall looked out onto the garden a story below, where the fighting had already spilled into the mazelike greenery. More Greencloaks fought amid the hedges and flower-covered cages, but for every one that won, two seemed to fall, and half of those rose again with vicious black marks across their foreheads. The infection was spreading. There were too many to fight.

There was nothing waiting for them down in the garden except more danger, but the garden was circled by a wall. Its top provided a ledge of ivy-covered stone. On the other side the wall gave way not to the castle, but to the city—and beyond that somewhere, the docks and the ship and the way home.

Only yesterday, Abeke had stared up at the masked stranger in red as he stood on that wall. Now she was climbing through a castle window and lowering herself onto it.

Rollan and Tasha followed. Uraza hesitated, and Abeke held out her arm, inviting the leopard back into her passive state, but Uraza refused and climbed out. Abeke didn't know if the gesture was a sign of protection or a mark of the weakening bond. The leopard padded along the wall with her usual grace, and Abeke was grateful for the gift of her feline balance, while the rest struggled not to fall. The rain was still only a drizzle, but it was enough to slick the tops of the stones on the courtyard wall. Tasha hadn't inherited Ninani's grace and nearly lost her balance twice, Rollan's hand flashing out to steady her before she tumbled over the side.

And then, halfway around the wall, a Greencloak below with a pulsing brand on his forehead saw them and hissed. He began to climb one of the trellises that ran from the garden floor. He moved with the steady fearlessness of the possessed, scaling the lattice and coming toward Abeke, when Essix dove.

The gyrfalcon raked her talons over the man's face. He went over the edge and didn't get back up.

"Good, Essix!" called Rollan shakily as they rounded the edge of the wall. "I love that bird."

One by one, they leaped to the stone street below.

Abeke and Uraza both landed in a crouch. Rollan dropped less gracefully over the edge, but still ended up on his feet. He turned to help Tasha down, but to their surprise, the girl landed and rolled. There was something almost—*almost*—graceful about it.

"Full of surprises," said Rollan, helping her to her feet.

Castle bells rang out overhead. When Abeke glanced back, craning to see, she thought she caught sight of a Greencloak in one of the higher towers—maybe Bern—summoning the infected, drawing their attention back into the castle and away from the young Greencloaks fleeing its walls.

There was a main road that ran from the castle to the docks, but that one was brimming with smoke and fire and fighting bodies. There were too many falling. Too many spiral marks.

"Rollan," said Abeke, "can you lead us?"

Rollan flashed an exhausted smirk and tipped his head back for an instant, eyes closed. His lips started to move, and Abeke leaned closer to hear what he was saying—*second left, third right, first right, third left*—as he tried to memorize the city. When his eyes flashed open again, he nodded, and they set out.

With Rollan's help—and Essix's bird's-eye view—they made it through the city without being seen, let alone overtaken. All around them, swords clashed and arrows flew on the streets. Beastly snarls and shrieks were woven in with the more human shouts. Uraza prowled at Abeke's side, ears twitching with the sounds of the falling Stetriol.

And then, somewhere between the main square and the docks, the storm *truly* broke.

Rain pounded the city, weighing down their cloaks and slowing their steps. The leopard growled in displeasure, but Abeke didn't care about getting wet. They were almost to the docks, and the ship, and safety. Rollan said something, but the downpour swallowed his voice. Abeke could hardly hear over the storm, so she didn't notice the steps closing in until it was too late.

The back alleys vanished behind them, the roads converged, and the last stretch of space before the docks was laid bare. The docks themselves were eerily empty. A dozen boats ran ashore—a mismatched array of skiffs and galleys and ships, devoid of crews, their ranks now on land, and tearing apart the city.

Abeke, Rollan, and Tasha raced as fast as they could. They were nearly to the mouth of the docks, the *Tellun's Pride II* in sight, when the infected finally fell upon them. They spilled like wasps out of the cracks to every side, a voiceless army of empty eyes and marked skin, puppets on someone else's strings.

Abeke was out of arrows, Rollan out of knives. Tasha's fists were clenched and shaking from shock.

The infected were a wall, a cage, closing in.

It wasn't fair. The ship was so close. It was right there, beyond a barricade of men and women and beasts.

And then, between a flash of lightning and the echo of thunder, she saw it.

A glimpse of red.

He came back, thought Abeke as the figure in the faceless mask vaulted into the fray.

And this time he wasn't alone.

A sea of crimson followed in his wake. A dozen masked figures, all in red, the others with the faces of dogs and cats, rams and boars and deer. They came with staffs and swords and daggers, and a few even seemed to have *claws*. They moved with inhuman speed and animal strength, slamming into the wall of enemies, forcing them back and carving a path to the ship.

"Go!" said the boy in the faceless mask.

And they did, lunging through the gap in the infected horde before it could close again. Essix soared ahead, landing on the ship's rail as the others raced down the dock.

"Worthy! Stead! Shadow!" called the stranger. Three of the red cloaks barred the path to the docks, holding the enemies at bay with blade and arrow.

Who were they? How were they so strong? The questions tangled in Abeke's head as they raced to the *Tellun's Pride II* and freed the ropes from their anchors on the dock. The tethers fell away and the kids clambered up the plank onto the deck. Together, Rollan and Abeke forced the wet canvas of the sails open, and the ship shuddered slightly as the fabric filled with storm wind.

But even as the sails filled, the ship didn't move.

It was caught on something, wedged by some unseen debris.

No, thought Abeke. *No, no, no, we're so close.*

As if he could read her mind, the figure in the faceless mask peeled away from the fight, leaping over the infected and the barricade of his own, and sprinting down the dock toward the ship.

He took up an oar, braced it against the hull, and pushed with all his strength.

"Please," called Abeke as the ship groaned and began to move. "Tell me who you are."

The stranger looked up and met her eyes.

"We are the Redcloaks," he said.

The ship slid free, jerking away as the wind caught the sails, and the stranger was gone, a blur of crimson back into the fray.

Thank you, she wanted to say, the words now lost with the rest of Stetriol.

The storm battered the water and caught up the ship, dragging it out into the bay.

Rollan leaned into the ship's wheel while Tasha stood at the side, gripping the rail and watching her home crumble.

Abeke stared, too, feeling numb. What had an hour before been a vibrant city filled with fireworks and celebration was now a city plunged into madness and panic.

All those new buildings, thought Abeke. *All those fresh trees.*

A cry went up overhead, and she craned her neck to see a bird perched atop the mast. At first she thought it was Essix, but then lightning lit the sky and she saw the parrot's colorful plumes. Relis!

Abeke was about to call up to the captain's bird when she heard the creak of racing steps, too late. Essix screeched in warning and a shout went up—Rollan's—from the other side of the ship, and then something lunged at Abeke, tackling her from behind.

She went down hard on the rain-streaked deck, her head hitting the wood and her vision crackling with light. And then it cleared, and she saw that the thing on top of her wasn't a thing at all, but a dark-skinned woman with short black hair. Her cloak—once green—was stained by smoke and dirt and someone's blood.

"Nisha," gasped Abeke as the woman wrapped her claw-like fingers around Abeke's throat. "Nisha!"

But it wasn't Nisha, not anymore.

Her dark eyes were empty, and the spiral twitched on her forehead with her pulse. A guttural sound escaped the woman's throat, but nothing more. None of the captain's orders. None of the cheerful banter. Only a hollow rasp. The parrot circled, and cried, unwilling to abandon her fallen captain, unwilling to attack in her stead.

On the deck, Abeke tried to fight Nisha off, but she had no strength left. Her head was pounding from the blow, and she couldn't breathe, let alone scream as a parasite crawled down Nisha's arm toward the hands wrapped around Abeke's throat.

A growl tore free, but it didn't come from her or the infected captain.

Uraza loped across the deck and fell on Nisha, tearing the woman backward by the hood of her cloak. The leopard held fast, shaking her from side to side before throwing her back into the ship's rail, where she lost her balance and went over. Nisha clawed at the air, but it was too late. She plunged down into the churning water, came up, choking and growling, and then went under.

Abeke gasped for air, got to her feet, and found Rollan struggling with another infected, one she recognized with sick despair. Arac. Arac, who had stayed on the ship with his captain, his wife, and fallen alongside her. The black spiral pulsed on his forehead above empty eyes.

"A little help!" choked Rollan as he fought to hold the man back. Tasha came stumbling forward—the swaying ship doing nothing to improve her balance—a bundle of coarse rope gathered in her arms. She tossed the net over the man. He thrashed like a fish, knotted up in the cords, and Rollan shoved him away. The ship rocked and Arac went rolling backward, a tangle of limbs that plunged over the edge and into the churning black water.

For a second, no one moved, every one of them coiled, braced for another attack. But neither Nisha nor Arac climbed back aboard.

At last, Rollan's legs buckled, and he sat down hard on the deck.

Essix landed on the wet boards, missing several feathers.

Tasha stood shivering, her back against a crate.

Abeke leaned hard against Uraza's damp fur.

She scoured the storm-black skies for the parrot, but he was gone.

No one spoke.

They were alive. They had escaped. But it could not be called a victory.

The rain was falling hard now, dousing the many fires, but it wasn't enough to stop the damage or save the people who had fallen. Abeke turned back and watched Stetriol shrink in the distance until nothing was left but smoke and sea.

17

NEWS AT SEA

THE *TELLUN'S PRIDE II* LOOKED LIKE A GHOST SHIP, DRIFT-
ing through the mist-laced morning.

A vessel fit for a crew of thirty Greencloaks, it now held
only three.

Rollan sat on the ship's dock, his back against the wheel,
his head bobbing with fatigue. Essix perched on a bundle
of rope beside him, preening her wet feathers. Abeke and
Tasha were curled up on a tarp nearby. Rollan had found
a spare green cloak and wrapped it around Tasha's trembling shoulders, and the two girls had collapsed as soon
as the city was out of sight.

Uraza had retreated into her passive state after only an
hour at sea, when the sloshing of the ocean and the per-
sistent rain became too much for the leopard, leaving the
three humans and Essix drifting toward home. Whether
it was the fear of another attack, or the memory of Nisha
and Arac and the rest of the crew left in Stetriol, none of
them had been willing to go belowdecks. Instead they'd
stayed above, braving the last of the weather. They shivered,

but not from cold, and even though it went unspoken, Rollan thought they all needed the rain to wash away what had happened that night.

Now, every muscle in his body hurt. Even the ones he didn't know he had. He bore a split lip and more bruises than he could count. He hoped that, wherever Meilin was, she was having an easier time.

He kept a list in his head of all the things he'd tell Meilin when he saw her again. He spent the long hours of the stormy night trying to decide how he would recount Stetriol, not just the battle, but the changes he'd seen in this land at the edge of Erdas: the little girl in the street, the laughter in the air, the mysterious fighters with their red cloaks and their animal masks. He was sure she'd have her own tales to tell.

Rollan yawned. The storm had passed before dawn, leaving only streaks of clouds in its wake, and as the sun finally rose, it turned the sky a bruised purple, then red, before finally showing the first signs of blue. A new day. His muscles begged for sleep, but his mind wouldn't let him rest. Every time he closed his eyes, Rollan saw Stetriol, its shape now lost from sight. He played it all back in his mind—the festival, the bond's strain, the attack—trying to figure out what was wrong.

Because something *was* wrong. About the night. About the battle.

It had been nagging at him for hours, a question, a name.

Zerif.

Where had the man been during the attack on the city? They'd faced his infected army in Stetriol, but not its leader, and while Rollan shuddered to think about what would have happened to them all if they'd had to face Zerif, too, with his stolen Great Beasts, it just didn't make sense.

Proud Zerif with his broad shoulders and his trimmed beard, his imperious voice and his cruel smile. Zerif was always at the center of his fights, taunting his opponents, calling out orders, relishing his victories.

But he hadn't been in Stetriol, and that made Rollan nervous, because if he wasn't in Stetriol, then where *was* he?

The bundle of green cloaks shifted on the deck beside him, and Tasha sat up, her white-blond hair, once neatly braided, now a messy, rain-curled nest around her head.

"Morning," said Rollan, trying and failing to keep the exhaustion from his voice.

"Where are we?" she asked, looking around. He realized that this girl had probably never seen the edges of her own city, let alone anything beyond.

"Well," said Rollan with a yawn, "we're somewhere between Stetriol and Greenhaven. I did pay *some* attention to Nisha when she was at the wheel. We don't have the whales, and the wind's not as strong, but I think I can get us home."

Home. The wrong word to use; he could see it in the pain that flickered across Tasha's face. Abeke stirred beside her, uncurling like a cat.

"What's it like?" asked Tasha, drawing her knees to her chest. "This Greenhaven?"

"It's a castle," said Rollan, "kind of like the one in Stetriol, only not as fancy." He tipped his head back against the crate. "It's more like a well-worn coat. Old stones and lots of green, but full of good people. You'll get to meet them all. And hopefully," he said, voice tightening, "hopefully our friends will be back by the time we arrive. Conor and Meilin. You would like them. But Olvan, he's the guy in charge, and he'll be there to welcome you . . ."

He couldn't tell if Tasha was still listening. Her gaze had drifted out to sea. She wasn't looking ahead, toward Greenhaven, but back, toward Stetriol.

"Did this all happen because of me?" she whispered.

"No," said Rollan firmly. "This happened because of Zerif."

Abeke wrapped her arm around Tasha's shoulders. "It will be okay," she said, and they all knew the words weren't enough. But they had to be said. Something had to be said.

Rollan chewed his cheek and then sat forward. "I studied the plans for Stetriol's castle," he offered. "Back in Olvan's rooms, before we left Greenhaven." Tasha looked up at this, but still said nothing. "There are hidden doors," he went on, "pathways in and out of the castle. Ones that lead away from the city, some to the docks, and some farther inland. I'm sure that some people in the east and west wings knew about those doors."

"How can you know?" asked Tasha.

"I can't," he said. "But I can hope."

Rollan looked up, past the sails at the brightening sky, and frowned at the sight of a bird soaring toward them. It wasn't his falcon—Essix was still perched beside him—or one of the gulls he'd seen closer to land, but a *raven*. Essix saw it, too, head swiveling, and then she was airborne, winging swiftly toward it. Rollan got to his feet, squinting as the bird drew near, and then Essix's screech tore through the air as she charged it, cutting off the raven's path, sharp talons forward. They struggled in midair, a tangle of wing and beak, before Essix sank her talons into the raven's wing.

"Essix!" he cried as the light caught the ribbon on the raven's dark ankle. "It's one of ours!" But it didn't make sense. Olvan used pigeons for messages. Why would he send a raven?

The falcon dove and deposited the raven rather roughly on the ship's deck before swooping to the rail and perching to watch.

The air caught in Rollan's throat.

It wasn't an ordinary raven.

It was Wikerus. His mother's spirit animal. But why would Olvan have used Wikerus? Was his mother at Greenhaven?

The raven struggled upright, fluttering his feathers indignantly as Rollan scooped him up, mumbled an apology, and freed the note from his foot.

Rollan's chest tightened.

The note wasn't from Olvan at all. It wasn't from Greenhaven.

The paper was bound with a yellow ribbon, and yellow meant *Lenori* at the Evertree. Rollan's chest ached at the thought of news, hope warring with fear. Had something happened? Why wasn't the message coming from Olvan himself? Why was his mother's bird so far from home? Had she gone to the tree? Or had Lenori borrowed the raven to send word? Rollan's fingers shook. Abeke was on her feet and beside him, one hand on his sleeve as he unrolled the slip to reveal the healer's small cursive.

Rollan's heart lurched as he read the words.

There was no mention of Conor, or Takoda, or Meilin.
Only three short lines.
Greenhaven has fallen.
Find Cabaro in Nilo.
Do not *return.*

GREENHAVEN
HAS FALLEN

THE GREAT HALL AT GREENHAVEN WAS THICK WITH FEAR and smoke.

The first poured from the people, and the second poured from the hearth, where someone had cast a sack of powder into the fire, hoping to slow the intruders down. It had not worked, of course, and now the Greencloaks stood gathered in the center of the smoke-filled hall, corralled like cattle.

The long wooden table that once ran the length of the hall had been shoved against one wall, clearing the great stone space. Zerif stood atop it, his chest bare beneath his dark cloak, watching as his men, his *hands*—for that is how he thought of those marked by the seal, an extension of his body, his will—surrounded the men and women of Greenhaven, blocking them in.

Not cattle, he thought.

Mice.

He could smell their defiance, mingled with their fear, and he could not wait to strip them of it. The Wyrm's mark—the raised spiral on his forehead—pulsed faintly, writhing under his skin. With its rhythmic beat, the whispers wound their course through his head, guiding him, not the way they guided his *hands*, for he was not a mindless slave. No, these whispers were like those of a king to his trusted knight. And soon, Zerif would be much more than that.

Zerif spread his arms wide.

"Greencloaks," he mused aloud. "The protectors of Erdas. The protectors of the Evertree. The protectors of the sacred bond between a human and a spirit animal. *Greencloaks*." He sounded out the word. "Always so eager to be in control. No wonder you fear the loss of it so very much."

He nodded at two of his *hands*, and the men dragged a Greencloak forward, one of his eyes swollen shut and blood running from his nose.

It was time to set an example.

Zerif let his arms fall back to his side.

"You all believe there is strength in being *chosen*," he continued, stepping down from the table. "But I believe there is strength in *choosing*. In taking." With a flick of his wrist, he produced a glass vial. Inside, two parasites squirmed, waiting for their hosts. "Summoning a spirit animal is not the only way to claim one." His eyes fell on the Greencloak. His collar had been torn open, revealing the tattoo of a bear across his chest.

"Summon your spirit animal," instructed Zerif.

The Greencloak spit on the hall floor between them. *"No."*

Zerif considered the man, the spit, the vial. "Start breaking bones," he said.

One of Zerif's *hands* wrenched the captive's arm behind his back, and the beginnings of his scream were cut off by Zerif's command.

"No," he said. "Not *his* bones." He scanned the gathering of Greencloaks, then pointed to another one of their ranks. "Hers."

Two more of his *hands* reached for the second Greencloak, a lean older woman. She twisted and fought, her colleagues trying to shield her, but Zerif's men managed to wrest her from the pack.

"You won't succeed," she growled as the infected forced her to her knees. "You never will."

Zerif ignored her. "Start with her fingers and toes," he instructed.

"Please," begged the man.

"Once you run out of bones," Zerif went on, "kill her."

"Stop!" said the man.

Zerif turned toward the man again, as if he'd forgotten he was there.

"If you want to spare her," he said simply, tipping one of the parasites from the vial onto his dagger, the wormy darkness squirming on the blade, "then summon your spirit animal."

"Don't, Alon," demanded the older woman. "It won't stop him."

"I said, start breaking bones."

"Wait!" shouted the man, Alon. A sob escaped his throat, but in a flash of light, the bear was there before him. It reared furiously, teeth bared, but before it could attack, Zerif plunged the dagger with its parasite into the bear's hide. Not a killing blow, of course; that would be a waste of such a splendid beast. The bear tore backward with a shudder and let out a single, strangled roar before coming down onto all four paws, the spiral pulsing in its forehead.

The man was still sobbing when Zerif took him by the jaw and tipped the second parasite into his mouth. The Greencloak struggled, but Zerif forced his hand over the man's lips. He felt the man fight the parasite's hold, watched the darkness creep like a vein up the man's cheek, around his eyes, before drawing its mark on his forehead.

When Zerif's hand fell away, the Greencloak knelt calmly, waiting for his orders.

One down.

Dozens to go. He turned back toward the woman, wondering who in the crowd she might care about. How tedious, to have to bend them one will at a time. Surely there was a better way.

He could feel the rising panic of the gathered Greencloaks, the murmurs of those desperate to fight back, and the soft protests of the others, terrified of what would happen if they tried.

"Listen close," he said, gesturing with his dagger. "You have a choice. Your future is your own to decide. You can die now by my hand, or you can serve at my side. And before you answer, remember that death is a very permanent decision. And you choose not only for yourself, but for your spirit animals. Your friends. Your family. Your Greencloaks. From this moment forward, if *any* of you refuse my offer, I will kill *everyone*."

Silence fell in the hall.

Zerif had learned in his many years that people were always willing to fight for their cause, and often willing to die for it, but rarely willing to condemn others to death.

"Now," he said with a cold smile, "who's next?"

They all knelt, in the end.

Most of them no doubt harbored some secret hope that they would be free again one day and seek revenge. Let them dream. Zerif didn't care *why* they knelt, or what they thought of as they surrendered, only that they did, swelling his ranks and cutting off the children's allies. By the time he was done, there would be nowhere to run and no one to run to.

And soon his *hands* would return from Stetriol bearing three more Great Beasts, and he would be one step closer. The whispers in his head grew louder in agreement, the hush of praise and pride washing over him, urging him on.

The Greencloaks of Greenhaven had all bowed to his will.

All except one.

A woman appeared at his shoulder, the spiral throbbing in her forehead.

"Have you found their leader?" he asked.

The woman tipped her head and pointed at the stairs to the northern turret. Holed up in his own chamber, then. Fear made such cowards of the weak.

As he crossed the courtyard, Zerif saw the bird taking wing from Olvan's chamber. A messenger.

One of Zerif's men nocked an arrow, but he held out a hand.

"Let it fly," he said with a menacing smile as he continued on. Let the old man spread the word while he still could. Greenhaven had fallen, and Zerif was winning.

Tethered in the corner of the courtyard was a moose. Olvan's spirit animal. An incredible beast. Zerif was planning to keep that one for himself, add it to his personal collection, if there was room. He drew a hand absently over his chest as he reached the tower, tracing the patterns of his collected army. *Gerathon. Rumfuss. Halawir. Suka. Arax. Dinesh. Tellun.*

He recited the names like an incantation as he climbed the stairs.

Gerathon. Rumfuss. Halawir. Suka. Arax. Dinesh. Tellun.

All his.

Zerif reached the landing outside the old man's chamber. Two of his *hands* stood guard beside the door, their expressions empty. There had been a time when Zerif wanted passion from his followers. Devotion. Belief. But those things had proved fickle. They could not be trusted. This—servitude—was the true way to power.

Zerif stepped forward and pressed his ear to the wood. Beyond, he could hear Olvan's scrambling steps, the scribble of his pen on parchment.

"A coward's choice, Olvan," said Zerif calmly, "to not stand with your men and women in the great hall. Not very leaderlike at all."

Olvan didn't answer, but Zerif could tell by the hesitation in his steps that he had heard.

"No matter," continued Zerif. "You are not their leader anymore."

He drew another vial from the pocket of his cloak and held it up to the light. Inside, the oily shape of the parasite shifted and slithered like a snail without its shell. From some angles, it looked like smoke, from others, like ink, or grease, or damp earth. It was none of those things.

It was darkness.

A sliver of the Wyrm, a seed set free to find fresh soil and take root.

"You will not win in the end, Zerif," came Olvan's voice through the wood. "I will not see it happen."

Zerif uncorked the vial and knelt, setting the glass on its side at the base of the door.

"It *is* the end," he said, "and I have already won."

The parasite slid—less like a worm than a snake—from the glass enclosure, vanishing beneath the door. "But you are right about one thing, Olvan. You will not see it happen."

He waited several long moments, and then, beyond the wooden door, at last, the sounds of struggle. A gasp. The crash as a metal pot and a pile of books were swept from a table, and moments later, silence.

Zerif could feel the new link, a pulse in his forehead as Olvan's will became his, and he smiled, knowing that he had claimed the leader of the Greencloaks.

He pressed a hand to the wood. "Open the door," he commanded.

The spiral twitched in his skin, met by the footsteps across the floor, the sliding of the bolt, the creak of the wood.

Zerif considered the old man, his gray hair, his strong eyes now empty. The great Olvan, nothing but a puppet now.

"Put him with the others," ordered Zerif. He stepped past the old man and into the chamber, eyes trailing over the wreckage of ink and pots. At the window he looked down on the courtyard, where his *hands* were gathering, their masses now mixed with figures in forest green. And for every man and woman, a beast.

They watched him, marked faces turned up, and waited for his orders.

Zerif turned away, and instead of going down to meet them, he went up, up a second set of stairs that led from the leader's chamber onto the battlements above.

From here, he could see the sea that stretched away, toward Stetriol, the hills of Eura, the mountains of Amaya. And even though he could not see the Evertree, he could feel its pull, or rather, he could feel the pull of the thing that lived beneath its roots, waiting to be free.

The wind caught Zerif's cloak, ran through his dark hair, brushed over the black tattoos that marked his tan skin.

Gerathon. Rumfuss. Halawir. Suka. Arax. Dinesh. Tellun.

He traced their patterns on his chest, his arms, felt where they wrapped around his ribs and back. Their markings ran together, tail to claw, horn to wing, twisting over him like armor.

The whispers in his head began to coalesce, drawing together from many voices into one. A voice that rumbled and rustled and hissed. A voice that changed its shape as often as the parasite. The Wyrm was getting stronger, and so was Zerif.

And strength, like everything, had two sides.

A body had to be strong enough to face the dangers from without, *and* the trials from within. Too often people thought only of the outside threats. But what good was a body if it was strong enough to fight off attackers, but not *infection*?

What *was* a body, if not a shell, a conduit, meant to harness one's power, and express one's will?

Gerathon the Serpent.

Rumfuss the Boar.

Halawir the Eagle.

Suka the Polar Bear.

Arax the Ram.

Dinesh the Elephant.

Tellun the Elk.

Every beast made him stronger. Every beast brought him closer. The markings coiled and curved and charged across his skin. Even in their passive forms, he could feel their strength, their skill, their cunning. The talismans had given him gifts, but none so great as these. The Great Beasts woke to his command and slept against his skin.

He looked down and considered the stretches of unmarked skin.

There was room for more.

Room for Mulop the Octopus, and Cabaro the Lion.

Room for Ninani the Swan, and Kovo the Ape.

Room for Jhi the Panda, and Uraza the Leopard.

Room for Essix the Falcon, and Briggan the Wolf.

The spiral pulsed, and the whispers rose in a chorus, and beneath the roots of the Evertree, the Wyrm strained against its prison, longing to be free.

"Soon," said Zerif to the thing beneath the world. "Soon, I will be strong enough. Soon, I will be ready for you."

And then, thought Zerif with a wicked smile, *I will be unstoppable.*

Victoria Schwab is the author of nearly a dozen books for children, teens, and adults, including *The Archived* and *A Darker Shade of Magic*. When she's not wandering the Scottish countryside or huddled in a French cafe, she's curled up in her Nashville home with two big dogs and two noisy cats, drinking tea and dreaming up monsters.

BOOK THREE:

THE RETURN

Split between two worlds, the team races to stop an
ancient evil. Above, Abeke and Rollan infiltrate an
impenetrable fortress to rescue the Great Beast
within, while below, Meilin and Conor find themselves
adrift in a vast underground ocean.

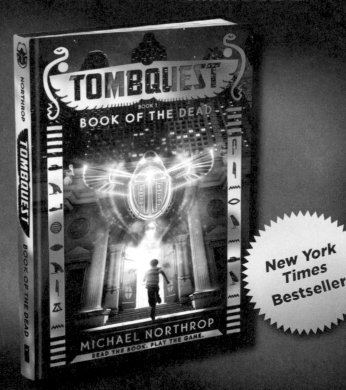